I0557519

The Heart of Seras
The Elders

The Heart of Seras: Book Two

Joe Evener

Published by **Rogue Phoenix Press**
Copyright © 2015

ISBN: **978-1-62420-222-3**

Credits
Cover design by Designs by Ms G
Editor: Amando Roberts

Dedication

Thank you to all of my family, friends, and supporters who have continued to encourage me through this process. You all rock, and I hope you enjoy book two as much as you enjoyed the first one! Thank you Bronwen, once again, for all of your love and support as I follow this dream wherever it may lead.

Five are the Elders with their gifts born in the black of night.
Five are the Elders' gifts hidden to set Seras right.
Five Elders pitted beneath an angry sun.
Blood will flow. Flesh and blade become one.
The Blood is given to ease time;
The Breath known to free men's minds;
The Bones to merge distance and space;
The Body a destined warrior, the Solia Custor, out of place,
Forged in battle with one true oath –
Protect Tolth's final gift, the Heart of Seras, our final hope.
~ Ancient Seras Prophecy

God stood in the congregation of the mighty; in the midst of the gods He rendered His verdict.

"How long will you judge unjustly, and show favoritism to the wicked? Defend the poor and fatherless! Do justice to those who are oppressed and suffering! Deliver the poor and needy! Free them from the hand of the wicked! They neither know nor understand. They stumble about in darkness; all the foundations of the world crumble."

Then He said, "You are gods. All of you are children of the Most High. But now you shall die like mortals and fall like men."
~ Recorded in part by Asaph in Psalms 82

Chapter One

"Jules, rise and shine, sweetheart," the baritone voice of Julie Ayers' father, Phil, carried up the steps and through Julie's closed door. Julie shook her wavy brown hair. Waking up was the last thing she wanted to do. A little more than a month had passed since her birthday…since the day she watched Callista the Hemoor warrioress die. Every day since then had been a struggle. She had skipped all of her non-mandatory cheer practices and open gym basketball practices. All she wanted to do was lie in bed and cry.

"Come on, we're going to be late," he said. She could hear her parents' conversation at the bottom of the staircase.

Today was the town of Sunset's Fourth of July celebration. The parade, the flea market, games at the high school and fireworks were a staple in every Sunset citizen's life. Julie wanted no part of it.

"I swear she's still mad at us for leaving her on her birthday," her mother said, and Julie could hear the sound of her mother beginning to walk up the steps.

"You can't blame her. She'll come down when she's ready."

At least dad gets it.

"Phil, that was a month ago."

Julie sat up, wiped the sleep out of her brown eyes and dropped her feet to the floor. *Fine. I hate this.* She stood up in a huff. "I'm coming!" she yelled down to her mother and father. *I can't stand to hear my parents argue.*

"Um, Julie, okay. We'll wait for you in the car while you get ready," her father said.

She heard the front door close. Julie slowly moved across the room to her closet to grab some clothes. *I wish I could talk to somebody.* She pulled a t-shirt over her head. *Who am I going to tell? Claire? She would never understand. Mom or Dad? They think I'm still mad about them going to Europe without me…which I am a little. Mr. C.?* She finished the conversation with herself by hopping into a pair of shorts and sliding on her running shoes. *No, I am never talking to him again. It's his fault anyway. He took me to Seras. He made me fight in that stupid battle. It's his fault Callista got killed by that freaking seven-foot giant.* She placed her hands over her eyes and blew out a deep breath then she wiped the pooling tears from her eyes. *No, I am never going to talk to him ever again.*

She lethargically walked down the staircase and out the door. Her parents were waiting as they promised.

"Are you sure you want to go?" Michelle asked.

"Yes. Why are you asking me that now?"

"You don't have to, honey," Phil said.

"Yes, I do. You already got me up and I can't stay here all day."

"I'm glad you're going," her mom added as Julie closed the door of their minivan and buckled her seatbelt.

Julie and her family, minus her brother, Patrick, made the short drive from their cozy, country home to town. They drove by the rows and rows of cornfields.

"Knee high by the Fourth of July," Julie's father said, quoting an old wives tale or wise tale, Julie could never figure out which.

They crossed over the pebble-stoned bridge that crossed over Cedar Creek. This was the same spot that she and her family were driving a little less than three years ago when the mysterious naked man appeared out of nowhere in front of her father's metallic blue Nova. Only later did she find out that the naked man was Mr. Marcus Campbell, her ninth grade English teacher, even though he wasn't a real teacher at all but a warrior sent from another dimension, Seras, to find her. "Boy, has my life changed," she whispered.

"What's that dear?" her mother asked.

"Nothing, I just said we're here."

On one of the hottest days of summer, the small village of Sunset, Ohio was buzzing with the excitement of the holiday season. It was the Fourth of July, Independence Day. Cars were lined up on both sides of the street on every road leading to town.

Her dad found a parking space in the grass of the school's softball outfield.

"Are you going to find your friends?" her father asked.

"Nah, I'll watch the parade with you. If that's okay?"

"It certainly is, young lady." Her dad put his arm around her and tussled her hair.

Sunset's parade consisted of an array of tractor pulled floats for churches, scout troops, and other local clubs; horse riders showed off their beautiful animals; hot rod cars carrying the mayor, the fall homecoming queen, the winter homecoming queen, local politicians, and the parade's Grand Marshall—a comely news personality. Sprinkled into the mix on the hot July day were various organizations, sports teams, and boys and girls riding patriotically decorated bicycles. Every float threw candy as hordes of children ran out to gather it up.

Everyone stopped to watch as older men carrying the flag of the United States of America, a Prisoner of War flag, and the State of Ohio flag walked past the crowd, the onlookers rose in honor of the flags and what they represented. Every man wearing a hat removed it, and many people placed their right hand over their heart.

Seeing the bright green and yellow uniforms of the Cedar Creek marching band lining up gave Julie a melancholy pause. School would be starting in another month and a half. "I really need to get my act together," Julie said aloud as she bent down to scoop up a handful of candy that had been tossed in her direction.

After the last fire truck went by, horns sounding and playfully spraying water at the crowd, a much-needed relief from the heat, Julie turned to her parents. "Hey, is it okay if I go find Claire?"

"Of course it is," her father answered.

"Cool. I'll see you later."

"Come find us before the fireworks. You know where we usually sit," her mother said.

"I will." Julie looked at her phone. Claire had sent a text about thirty minutes before that she had missed. She sent a message back that she was on the way.

She caught up with Claire and three other friends near the fountain on the town square. The girls squealed and hugged each other as if they had been gone for years.

"Where have you been hiding?" Claire begged. "You've been M.I.A. all summer."

"Yeah, Jules," one of the other girls agreed.

"I've been busy," Julie answered in a non-convincing way.

"Did ya forget about cheer camp?" Claire reminded her. "You haven't been to one, yet."

"Or basketball camp," a teammate from last year added.

"No, I haven't forgotten. Like I said, I've just been busy," Julie answered. The foursome began walking through the throng of shoppers at the flea market.

Julie and her friends stopped at a local vending booth selling homemade ice cream. "I'll take two scoops, please."

"What's his name?" Her best friend winked.

"I wish." Julie smiled. "I've been studying for my driver's test." It was only a partial lie. "My parents promised they would take me to get my license before school starts."

"That is so cool. I can't believe you'll be driving as a sophomore," one of the girls said.

"Yeah, but getting held back by an overprotective mother isn't all it's cracked up to be," Julie answered.

4

"Eww, yuck," they said in unison.

"Why did she do that?" another asked.

"I don't know," she lied, but it wasn't worth explaining to them.

"I just started my driving classes," Jimmy, Claire's boyfriend, joined the conversation as he brought Claire a fountain drink from another concession stand.

"Thanks," Claire said to Jimmy as they shared a quick kiss. "And don't worry, you haven't missed anything at the cheer camps. I'm not even sure why we need to go."

"Are you nuts? The new routines are impossible," one of their friends cried out.

"Maybe for you," Julie teased, starting to feel more ease.

The group laughed at the girl's expense.

"I'm just kidding."

"I know," the girl said. "But I do think they are hard." She shrugged.

"I think half of the town is here to watch the parade," Julie said, changing the conversation.

Jimmy smirked, "And the other half was in it."

"That's not nice," Julie squealed.

"But it's true." He ran his hand through his short cropped hair.

"Well, I'm glad you're here. Now we can get back to normal," Claire said.

"Trust me, I can't wait for things to get back to normal."

Julie and her friends continued to walk around the town square's brick-lined streets and well-groomed lawn before turning toward the high school and the carnival games that were spread across the school parking lot.

"Look, it's Mr. Langston," Claire said, pointing to a dunk tank with the popular history teacher perched precariously above the container of water.

"Oh, I want to throw a ball at him," Julie said with a confident swagger.

"Okay, how 'bout a contest?" Jimmy asked. "Whoever knocks him down with the least amount of throws buys…"

"Buys what?" Claire asked.

"Um…"

"Fries and a shake, duh!" Julie said.

"Deal," Jimmy answered.

"I'll sit this one out," Claire said.

"Sissy!" Julie chided.

Mr. Langston cleared his goggles. "What do we have here? There's no way you're going to knock me down."

"I'll go first," Julie said. She paid her money and grabbed three balls.

"Now, Julie, I know you can't hit the target. You're a cheerleader," Mr. Langston ribbed her.

"That does it," Julie said, wrinkling her nose and lips in determination. She threw once, a complete miss.

"You throw like a girl," Mr. Langston yelled as the softball missed its target. "See, you should do a real sport like track," he teased.

The next throw sent the beloved history teacher and track coach into the cold water with a splash. Julie leaped in the air. "Yes!" she screamed.

Jimmy went next. "To make it fair, I'll use my left hand." The two girls smirked. On his first throw, Mr. Langston tumbled into the water, again.

"How did you do that?" Julie and Claire squealed.

"It was easy, I'm bi-hand…ual."

"Don't you mean ambidextrous?" Julie corrected.

"Okay, ambi-handual," he joked. Julie and Claire simultaneously slapped their foreheads.

The three friends left Mr. Langston shivering as he climbed back into his seat. "I'll see you guys in forty-three days!"

"Aw, man!" Jimmy exclaimed. "Way to ruin the mood."

"Bye, Mr. Langston! See ya soon!" Julie yelled back then turned to her friends. "I can't believe school starts in forty-three days."

"That sucks," Jimmy said.

"Yeah, it does," Claire agreed.

A short time later they found a vendor, and as promised Julie bought Jimmy a shake and fries. Julie squirted extra vinegar on her order. "Mmm, a lemon shake and fair fries loaded with vinegar. I'm a happy girl," Julie said as she stuffed her mouth with the greasy treat.

"How do you stay so skinny?" Claire asked.

"Yeah, right," she protested.

"Yes, you are! You look good."

"Well, I've was working out pretty hard," she said, though not convinced of her friend's comments.

"Mr. Campbell must be a pretty good trainer," Jimmy said. "Maybe I should ask him to get me ready for football."

"Sure, go ahead," Julie said.

"Cool, I'll ask him when school starts up."

"You do that," she said with a tinge of sarcasm not meant for her friends, then shifted her attitude. "I'm sure he'd be glad to help. I have to go catch up with my mom and dad. I'll see you guys a little later." She left to find her parents preparing their spot on the football bleachers, where they sat every year to watch the annual fireworks display. *I don't want to hear that name again.*

Julie walked toward the stadium, carrying her tall plastic cup filled with lemon shake, and in the other hand a container of fries. She found her parents talking to a group of their own friends, catching up with what is happening in their lives. *Probably talking about their trip.*

"Oh, my goodness," one of her mother's friends said as Julie bounded up the metal bleachers. "Is this little Julie? My, she is all grown up."

"Thank you."

"I just bet you're breaking all of the little boys' hearts," the woman continued.

Julie blushed.

"Don't be modest, sweetie. You can tell your Aunt Susan all about it."

"Susan, stop it," a curly haired man said. "You're embarrassing her."

Julie blew a sigh of relief, glad that the conversation came to a halt. "Hey, can I go sit with Claire and Jimmy?" she asked.

"Sure, where will you be?" her mother asked, turning to her from a conversation with the people sitting next to them.

Julie politely acknowledged the people her parents were talking to then said, "By the hill in front of the teachers' parking lot."

"Have fun," her mother said.

"I will."

"And behave," Phillip added.

"I will." Julie rolled her eyes. Her father shook his head as she started to skip away.

The little gang of friends sat back on the side of the grassy hill. Even surrounded by her best friend and all of her other friends, Julie never felt so alone. As the sky burst with greens, reds and purples across the cloudless night, Julie fought hard not to think about where Mr. Campbell was or what he was doing; she just couldn't help herself.

After the thirty-minute fireworks show, the entire town of Sunset made their way from the parking lot and side streets.

"What did you think of the fireworks this year?" Julie's mother asked her as they drove home after the night's activities.

"They were okay," she answered, looking out of the minivan window into the dark void of the country night.

"I thought they lasted longer than last year's," her father added. "I think they get better and better."

"Yeah."

"Julie, are you sure everything is okay? You normally love the Fourth," Michelle finally asked, turning in her seat.

"Yep."

"I am sorry we left you for your birthday. I've apologized a hundred times."

Julie felt rage rise from her chest. "I don't care about that!"

"Then what's wrong with you?" her mother questioned.

"Nothing! Just leave me alone."

"Phil?" Michelle turned to her husband.

"Jules, we were just trying—"

"I know. I'm sorry. Life is just…ugh!" She knew they meant well, but how could they understand when she couldn't?

"Honey, you can talk to us," her father said in the dark of the warm July night.

"No, it's my problem."

"How 'bout if we invite Mr. Campbell over for dinner?" her mother asked.

"What? Why?"

"I don't know. He did a lot for you and we haven't seen him this summer."

"No. That won't help. Geesh!"

"I was just trying…"

"Well, don't." She bounced her body away from her mom and crossed her arms. The night's conversation was over.

~ * ~

Marcus Campbell peered through his living room window, waiting, wondering and hoping. Earlier in the day he had walked to the village square, hoping to see Julie. He thought it was his best chance to finally catch up with her. She proved to be elusive. After watching the parade and wandering through the crowd at the annual flea market, he gave up and made the short mile and a half walk back to his apartment.

"She will come back," he whispered to his loyal companion, Shakespeare. The cat purred and rubbed against his leg. "I miss her too." Shakespeare meowed at his owner. "You're right. No, she won't. I failed."

Chapter Two

"Where is she?" Argos, the commanding general of the departed immortal Bhjuda Heilshorn's army, listened to Redderick Bobo, the second of the Elders' immortals, roar. Redderick's rampage broke the hush as a new dawn rose through the green, red, and yellow leaves of their high mountain range fortress.

Freya the Oracle stood to confront the portly man who stood in front of the wooden meeting hall. "I assure you, Marcus will bring the Heart back as soon as possible."

Redderick placed his hands on his hips, revealing his potbelly through an unbuttoned sleeveless vest. "And where is Marcus? Where is the Solia Custor? I have been here for months and I have yet to see him or the Heart," he continued his fit of rage. His face turned red, matching the blotchy patches on his pale skin.

Seated around the sparsely decorated room to witness the out lash besides Argos and Freya were Pertheus, the loyal leader of Marcus's infantry; Griffus, the hulking commander of the war machines; and Jayna, the last known Tarrack.

"They will be here," Argos tried to explain in a tranquil manner. "Julie, the Heart," he interjected so that Redderick knew who he was talking about, though Argos was sure that somehow he did, "went through a very traumatic experience." He watched the ancient scribe stomp back and forth. "It may take Marcus a while to calm her down and bring her back." He knew Redderick's intentions were of a faithful emissary to the Elders, but his actions were those of a spoiled child.

"She was devastated by the death of Callista in the Battle of Yellow Fields," Freya added.

"As were we all," Griffus said.

"That is no excuse!" Redderick Bobo said, slamming his hand on the table. "Do you know who I am? These are difficult times. We need the Heart here, now. I wasted enough time just getting here. I must start her training."

"I thought it was Marcus's job to train her?" Freya asked. Her long brown hair was wrapped with bright orange and green sashes and she wore a burnt orange gown.

"He is to teach her the way of the sword. I am to teach her everything else she needs to know."

"Which is?" Freya questioned.

"Which is for her to know," he answered as he looked at her with indignation. "Why is she allowed to come and go as she pleases?" Redderick's voice was more controlled now, though still displeased.

"Marcus wanted her to have her freedom," Pertheus jumped in to answer.

"Then where is Marcus? I have not seen him since I arrived. Does he want his freedom too?" He puffed out his chest, causing his potbelly to stick out even further than before.

Griffus scratched his thick blonde beard. "She is just a girl." He remained seated due to the damage his leg suffered in the battle.

"That is an unacceptable answer!" Redderick looked keenly on the present council. "This is not the way Tolth would have wanted it."

"Then maybe Tolth should not have chosen a girl of fifteen to do his bidding," Freya responded in anger.

"That is blasphemous!" The immortal stormed out of the council lodge.

"What do you think he is going to do?" Pertheus asked as all four leaders sat silent for a moment after the verbal attack.

"I am not sure what he is capable of," Freya said.

"I will keep an eye on him," Argos said.

"As will I," Jayna added.

The group left the meeting hall. The air was crisp and cool. The night time patrol protecting the outer perimeter huddled around the warmth of glowing fires as they waited for the morning change of the guard.

Argos mounted his steed. "We can only hope Marcus returns soon," he told his comrades, "or Redderick will only get worse."

"That is a pleasant thought," Pertheus said in a joking manner.

The village was beginning to wake. The townspeople lumbered out of the thick wooden doors of their sturdy houses of timber and rock. Wood window flaps were raised to let the fresh air into the cabin.

"We need to get Marcus back," Jayna said.

"Until he comes back, we are at Bobo's mercy," Griffus added. "He needs to know."

Freya patted him on the shoulder. "I imagine he will find out soon enough." She turned to Jayna. "May I have a word with you?"

The Tarrack woman bowed in respect as the group dispersed.

Argos watched as one by one they made their way back to their homes. Griffus stopped by a fenced area for livestock and a garden that flanked his and nearly every dwelling to ignite a fire in the stone circle made for cooking and warmth in the brisk early morning air. His wife, Laila, kissed him as she made her way to the marketplace in the center of town. Argos, husband of the village matriarch, Gwendolyn, and father of three fine warrior sons, Julius, Jakob, and Edwin, paused for a moment as if to visualize something before spurring his horse and heading for home.

~ * ~

Redderick marched into the large tent his servant, Charlena, had erected with help from the townspeople of Allon on the northeast side of the fortress village. It was adorned in vivid colors of majestic purple, royal blue, deep orange, and vibrant yellow.

Cushions were aligned on the floor as chairs, couches, and a single large bed. He glanced at the five women of his harem. He turned to the sandy-haired servant he despised. "You are dismissed, cow." He waved his hand, relieving her of her cleaning duties.

"Wait," he commanded his slave. "I have a job for you, and do not mess it up. Fetch me a cloak of the girl they call Julie," he ordered.

"Aye, sir," Charlena answered before excusing herself.

The chubby, red-headed Redderick took off his sleeveless vest, revealing his pale blotchy chest and oversized stomach, as the five beautiful women pranced over to him.

He kissed the red-headed woman passionately. "Ah, Meira, you taste like honey." Then he did the same with each of the other four. Teagon, a well-endowed blonde; Ehran, a long-limbed dark skinned woman with straight raven black hair; Lillian, another blonde; and Damaris, a light-brown skinned woman with springy dark brown hair. He then went back to Meira, kissed her again, and said, "Yes, yes, you will do just fine."

The other four left the tent as Redderick pulled Meria to join him on the large cushioned bed.

~ * ~

Queen Pallanex's screech resounded across the trimmed bush-lined paths of Cauleta. The guards stood in their positions on high alert as she approached the courtyard. The queen stormed past the empty white marble bases with the former occupants' figures crumbled in a rubble heap until she came to the statues still intact. She moved past those of herself, William, Kralen, Reinwald, and Eryx to the one of her late husband. She glared at the final figure in front of her. "Canis!" she growled at the image. "I would love nothing more than to rip you down with my bare hands so you could join those of your useless brother, the cowardice Elders, and your demonic-spawned son!"

She entered her chamber room, which glistened in its white décor, ordinated with gold and silver designs—a far contrast from the dark towers surrounding the palace and the exterior facade of the castle walls. The queen pushed open the dark redwood doors that matched the interior table, chairs, and wall hangings. The cushions of the seats were of royal blue fabric laced with gold thread. In a corner, sitting at an angle, was a long bench chair.

The news of General Areaq's return demanded her full attention. She walked briskly down her private staircase and past a display of three mummified soldiers where countless spiders had made their home. A spot for a missing relic was open. She gathered herself for a moment, smoothing her straight black hair lined with blue streaks that framed her long thin face.

"General," Queen Pallanex acknowledged. The stout man stood in respect and fear. "You look tired."

"My queen," he said, humbly. Areaq's arms revealed his matching tattoos of open jaws with row upon row of jagged teeth on his biceps.

"Is it true that you were the only survivor?"

"It is, my queen. Sadly…"

Before the conversation could go beyond mere pleasantries, William burst through a rustic exterior door that led to the back of the courtyard where the queen had guests of lesser importance enter. "Well, well, well, I heard you came back," William said.

"William!" Queen Pallanex scolded.

"Wait, someone is missing. Where is your partner, you know, the tall one?" His voice sang sarcastically.

"William, that is enough!" Pallanex roared.

"I would have much rather been defeated in battle than chase a myth," Areaq cackled.

"So you faced Marcus?"

"No."

"I did not think so. Otherwise you would not be standing here." William put his hand over his mouth as if just realizing something. "Is that what happened to your partner?" William asked, mocking the general with a sly undertone. "He was not…eh hmm, man enough to handle Marcus and you ran a like a coward?"

"I said that is enough!" Queen Pallanex ordered. She knew what had happened to General Juta. She also knew Areaq abandoned his position in the back of a wagon where he rested most of the night, detached his horse from the cart, and fled once the convoy was attacked coming through the mountain pass. "I did not invite you to this meeting," she said with disdain.

"We need to discuss that later. For now, I want to know where Marcus is and if Redderick is with him?" He whipped his head back to Areaq.

"William, I will ask the questions!" Pallanex demanded.

"We had been marching for too long," General Areaq said. "They ambushed us."

"Likely story," William scoffed.

"How did your search for the myth turn out?" Areaq snapped back.

"I assure you, Redderick is no myth," William said calmly and eerily out of character.

"Then where is he?" Areaq looked around in mockery.

The two generals stood in anger. Areaq drew his weapon.

"Sheath your sword, fool, before you impale your worthless hide on it." The intensity of William's eyes was just frightening enough to make the large general place his sword back into its leathery home.

"I am not taking abuse from this monster." Areaq pounded his hands on the wooden table in protest.

William slammed a dagger into Arcaq's hand, stared deeply into the general's eyes, cocked his head, and whispered menacingly, "Who are you calling a monster?"

"William, you are excused." Queen Pallanex's voice was now deep and foreboding. "I will not say it again."

William growled in anger. He turned his attention to Queen Pallanex but aimed his statement toward Areaq, "I am bored and I really need to kill something."

"The immortal is with Marcus," Pallanex said with confidence.

"How do you know?" he responded, still with a firm grip on the blade jammed in Areaq's hand.

The queen knew Areaq's body was in a state of shock. His eyes watched in horror as the blood drained from his hand, but he was too paralyzed to move or scream.

"Remember, I was the one who warned you about Marcus changing—"

"Stop!" William barked.

"And I am right about Redderick," she finished. "Gather your army; I have another mission for you."

"I have no army left," William grumbled, "thanks to this fool."

"Then find another one since your other army is not ready, yet."

"Sending me away on these little trips is delaying our plans," William seethed.

"You have your orders." Queen Pallanex dismissed the angry commander. William pulled the dagger out of the general's hand and left in a fit of rage.

The queen heard William curse, "By Azahleah's beast I will kill them all!" as he flung the thick door closed and mounted his horse. The sound of hoof beats echoed through the courtyard of statues.

Areaq wrapped a cloth around his punctured hand; the sting of William's blade had left it immobile. "That damned demon," he grumbled. "I wish he and all his kind would die."

"Now, now, general, no need to worry about William. He will not be bothering you anymore." Queen Pallanex leaned into the round muscular warrior. At full height, Areaq only came up to her neckline. For an instant she knew he thought she was going to kiss him.

He looked at her with the same lust men had done all of her life. Was he imagining her in the beauty of her youth? The legend of the young tribal servant who seduced the great Canis was well known throughout the land of Seras. Just as she got nose-to-nose with the general, she pulled away, leaving him anxious. "Tell me, general, did you see Marcus or the so-called Heart of Tolth?" Queen Pallanex purred.

"No, my queen. My position was too far back to see anything before the attack."

"I see. Would you like a drink, general? It is one of a kind."

"My lady, I have had drinks across all of the lands of Seras," he bragged.

"You have never had a drink like this," the queen cooed.

She poured a drink from one of the bottles on a side table into a fancy glass; its burgundy color sparkled as she swished it around slightly. She took a large drink but did not swallow. She swept her long black hair with blue streaks away from her face and moved closer to the anticipating man.

He opened his mouth and she did the same.

Queen Pallanex pressed her lips against his. The warm liquid drizzled down his throat and some on his beard.

Areaq caught his breath long enough to gulp the fluid down. It would not take long until he noticed a tingling sensation starting in his neck and working its way to his head and down his arms. "The pain in my hand is leaving. I like th…is…mag…ic," he barely coughed out.

With his eyes wide open, Areaq was frozen from the neck up. The poisonous liquid had not reached his lower torso, yet.

The queen leaned back and began moving him toward the rocky stairwell.

Queen Pallanex watched as Areaq tried in vain to walk. He tried to move, tried to speak, all to no avail. She smiled, knowing that the short general's mind could not comprehend what she was doing to him.

She assisted him up the first four steps and stopped him before his body lost all feeling.

"If you did not see Tolth's bastard child, you are useless to me, general." Queen Pallanex maneuvered his body backward into the open spot among the cobwebbed mummified soldiers.

Areaq's eyes were locked frozen on the queen. Like so many men before him, he realized his mistake in trusting her. But as was the case with all the others, it was too late. Only one had ever survived her poisonous attack, and even her late husband did not live long enough to tell anyone about her venomous deceit.

She took a hooked blade from a resting spot on the framed wall and glided it down the white encasing of the nearest mummified soldier's wrapping.

Thousands of the queen's eight-legged companions crawled from their former nesting spot and made their way to their new fleshy home and meal. Areaq's eyes flitted in horror at what was happening to him.

His mind screamed in terror, but no sound amplified from his infested mouth.

Chapter Three

"Oh, my gosh!" Julie said, "You've gotta love being a girl and having sweat gather on every fatty part of your body."

Claire and the other cheerleaders, dressed in shorts and sports bras, laughed as they took a time out to get a drink.

"I'm serious. I have sweat pouring from every possible pore. It looks like I just got out of a pool," she continued her humorous protest.

"Come on ladies," their instructor bellowed. "Football season is only three weeks away."

"Yuck. That means school is only three weeks away," Julie whispered.

The two dozen girls took their places on the high school's track and went through their paces in the hot summer sun.

"Who are you and what have you done with my best friend?" Claire asked.

"What?"

"The Julie I know loves school."

Julie shrugs. "I don't know, I guess I'm over it." She was lying to Claire, but she couldn't tell her that she was really concerned about not being able to avoid Mr. Campbell once school started.

"Okay," Claire drug out.

"Maybe I'll change my mind once it starts back up."

"Ladies, focus!" the cheerleading advisor broke in.

The music started and they moved in unison to the newly learned dance routine.

Later that day, Julie bounded upstairs to her room. She flung the door open with a new sense of energy. Cheerleading had been productive and she felt happy, the happiest she had felt in a long time.

She quickly grabbed a pair of cotton shorts and a t-shirt then made a giant leap from her bedroom door to the tiled floor of the bathroom. She took a much-needed shower after a long day of cheerleading practice. After the shower, she toweled off, got changed and made it from the bathroom to her bed in three long jumps.

"New world record!" she yelled. "Take that, Mr. Langston." Then Julie changed her tone, "Better not say that too loud or he'll try to recruit me again."

Julie laid her head down on her comfy beanbag pillow. The coolness of the soft beaded cushion helped put her right to sleep.

In the foggy mist of her mind's eye she saw swirls of red, white, and brown. A voice called out to her.

"Heart, come back to Seras. Come back to Seras, my Heart."

She tossed and turned, trying to block out the man's voice and his haunting request. So much for a good night's sleep.

~ * ~

A few weeks later, there was a familiar knock on Marcus Campbell's front door. Shakespeare was perched against the glass pane in excitement.

Marcus came out of the kitchen from making himself a cup of hot tea and opened the door; before he could get a single word out of his mouth the small frame of Julie stormed past him in a huff.

"What are you doing to me?" she yelled.

"I don't—"

"Don't give me that. I haven't slept in weeks," she continued loudly.

"Um, Julie, I haven't done anything," he desperately tried to explain.

"Well, whatever you're *not* doing, stop!" she screamed; then her tone changed. "Hi, Shakespeare," she hummed, picking up the happy white cat. "I've missed you. Yes, I have," she said, rubbing her nose against the cat's nose.

"Julie," Marcus dared breaking her focus on Shakespeare and experiencing her wrath, again. "I promise I have not done a thing to—"

"Stop. I'm not talking to you."

At that moment, Marcus debated with himself on why he had wanted to talk to her for the past two months.

Julie put Shakespeare on the floor and plopped down on Mr. Campbell's couch.

"Would you like anything to drink?" he asked as he attempted to change the subject and walked toward his tiny kitchen. "I have some hot tea on the stove."

"No, thank you," Julie said politely but with a snarky tone. "How about some juice or milk," she asked.

"Sure." He opened the refrigerator and noticed he was out of both. "Because, I don't have either of those things." He dropped his head in defeat and ran his hand through his brown hair.

"Don't worry about it. I'm not thirsty. I just want you to put an end to these nightmares."

"Julie, I promise I am not doing anything."

Well, something…or someone is killing my sleep."

"What?" He sat on the couch beside her. He leaned down, placed his elbows on his knees and clasped his hands in front of him.

"I don't know, but it's different than before."

"Before?"

"Yeah, the dreams I had about Seras before I went there."

"You never told me about those?"

"Yes, I did!"

"I would have remembered. What do you see?"

"The new ones or the old ones that I already told you about?" She bobbed her head back and forth sarcastically.

He decided to drop the topic of old dreams, happy to finally have her back, even in her current temperament. "The new dreams. We can talk about the old dreams later."

"It looks swirly and I hear a guy's voice."

"What does this guy's voice sound like?" he asked, worried William had somehow found Julie and discovered some way to manipulate her dreams, or worse, that he found a way to get to Earth, much like Rinna the Death Walker did last Halloween.

"I don't know." She shrugged. "He sounds old."

"What does he say?" Marcus was relieved that it wasn't William, but he was still concerned about someone from Seras entering her dreams.

"He keeps telling me to go back to Seras." Julie wrinkled her mouth to one side of her face.

"I have to agree." Marcus half-heartedly smiled.

"No way! I am never going back," she responded, crossing her arms like a spoiled child.

"Then why are you here?" he asked, more impersonal than he intended.

"To make my dreams stop," she barked. Julie picked Shakespeare up and placed him on her lap.

"I can't do that," he argued back.

"Then who can?" She tightened her lips and frowned.

"I don't know," he said. "I haven't been back to Seras since that night."

She paused unexpectedly. "What? Wait? Why not?"

"I…" Marcus stuttered.

"Whatever," she huffed. "I just want you to find out who's doing it and make the dreams stop." Julie rose from the couch.

Marcus stood firm. "I can't do that," he answered once again.

Julie gave him an expression like he just slapped her in the face. "Then you're out of luck," she said as she moved to the door to leave. "By the way, you didn't even ask how I got here," she goaded. "Yeah, that's right, I got my license. Not that you care." Julie bent down and stroked Shakespeare a final time before opening the door and slamming it behind her.

"You really didn't give me time," he whispered to nothing but air. "You also didn't let me tell you how badly the death of Callista affected me, too, or that I just wanted to make sure you were okay." Then he looked down at his cat who appeared to be judging him. "Oh, shut up."

~ * ~

Julie got in her mother's minivan. She turned the key to start the engine and then stopped. Her mind continued to race with thoughts and questions. *How long had it been since I last saw Mr. C.? More than a month? That's the longest I had been without him, my teacher...the fake teacher. Wow, things have certainly changed since I met him.*

She put the car in reverse and backed out of the parking spot. "Less than a year ago I was just a freshman, and he was just a teacher." Julie adjusted the gear to drive and pulled out of the apartment complex. *It's funny, on Earth we were nearly inseparable, and in Seras we rarely saw each other.* She had successfully avoided him since the night on the porch, the night she watched Callista die. *What was I thinking?*

Chapter Four

Flames flickered high above the archway held up by stone pillars. The rotten smell of sulfur permeated the air.

Inscribed across the smooth black stone was the warning: *The Soul of All Who Enter Shall Taste Death.*

"Oh, William," Queen Pallanex cooed. She peaked through the closed curtains of her carriage as a team of four massive black horses pulled it through an ice covered passageway of William's fortress, Shadowmor. "Why do you live in such filth?" The animals' breastplates were silver adorned with bronze studs. The regal carriage was constructed of reddish brown hardwood, which was masterfully sculpted with intricate drawings of royal scroll patterns and spider web designs embedded into the frame. The interior and curtains were made of violet crushed velvet.

The driver cracked a whip to hurry the team past the barren fields, across the moat bridge, and through the archway. On the face of the headstone was the emblem of a large bull with long horns.

"Whoa." The carriage came to a stop when the servant pulled hard on the reins. He scrambled from his perch to open the door. "My queen."

Queen Pallanex glided out, taking the hand of her assistant. She was wearing a thick red winter robe with a blue-dyed fur collar. Underneath, a tightly drawn green gown cut deep down the back and was laced with leather cord. Bronze bracelets decorated her arms, chained jewels dangled from her ears, and a circlet of gold looped around her dark, braided hair.

She looked up at the front of the building and its high arched walls against the gray haze-filled sky with rumbling blue clouds hovering overhead. "Wait here."

"Aye, my lady. And, may I ask, where are the guards?"

"I can only imagine, my dear, but anyone foolish enough to attack him is foolish enough to die."

Queen Pallanex could not see much beyond the dull light let inside by the opening of the door. The torches hung unlit in their iron holders on "T" shaped rock pillars. The cauldrons had been extinguished. Empty chains lingered against the lonely walls. The only other light was illuminating from small barred windows, along with a cold breeze from the gray sky outside.

The Queen looked around, disgusted by her surroundings. The heels of her boots reverberated across the slab floor to a set of stairs. She glanced up at the remnants of an old tower stairwell. She made her way to the top and opened the chamber door.

The area was nearly bare. Three semi-round pillars were protruding from the two abrasive walls away from the door and far window. Only a rack adorned with the black and purple cloak of the Skorei general, a ceramic jug and cup sat atop of a rickety table, and a large bed frame with a thick downy-stuffed mattress between four thick posts filled the room.

William sat on a stool behind a pillar. Her movement interrupted what he was doing. A pan of food clattered on the floor.

"Hello," he started, rising quickly from his seated position. "I was not expecting you." He was wearing black pants and shirt. His long dark hair flowed across his shoulders and down half the length of his back.

"How is your pet?" she asked with a tinge of anticipation.

"He is fine." Something scrambled into hiding through a chamber wall.

"Can I see him?"

"No," he growled. He stood in her way with his long raven locks flowing freely. He slid a hand through his hair, using his fingers as a comb.

"I insist," Queen Pallanex said, trying to look around his shorter frame. "Or should I order you?"

William hit her with a solid backhand. Her head jerked to the side with the force.

"I hope you enjoyed the two messengers I sent you?" Queen Pallanex slapped him in return; her face flush from his strike.

"I did…we did." A trickle of blood dripped from the side of his mouth.

"Good," she laughed. Her face, normally lined with age, smoothed at the excitement.

"Next time send them together. We were getting hungry." He grabbed her by the throat and pinned her back against the coarse wall.

"I did not mean for you to eat them."

"Why else would you send me two gifts?"

"They were supposed to give you the message that I was coming."

"They did." William smiled.

"I hope they put up a fight." The queen yanked off William's shirt.

"Just enough to work up an appetite." He pulled a dagger from her hair that had been pinning it up. Her tresses fell down the length of her back. "Enough foreplay," he rumbled. They kissed hard and his mouth moved from her lips to her neck.

"Is your army ready?" Queen Pallanex asked.

"No. I have been a little distracted."

She drew him closer. "You must focus."

"I am trying," he said, pressing her back into the wall harder. "Now, shut up."

"You need to head south."

William chuckled with a soft exhalation.

"There is an army being established south of the Linsay River," the queen arched into him, revealing her neck for his pleasure.

"The Linsay? In Hawkmir? Artavious is dead."

"The Hawkmir is rebuilding. It has been years since you and Marcus defeated them and killed King Artavious. You need to take your men and squelch any chance for a rebellion."

"My men? I have no men!" He threw her in anger onto the bed. "Remember, your foolish general destroyed most of my army." He shredded her dress from the back by pulling on the seams. "Where is your loyal general now?"

"I dismissed him," she told him as she tossed him on his back and straddled him.

"The worthless dog. I was wondering how long he would last."

"Fail me again and you will be next," she warned.

William rolled her onto her back. "I never fail!"

She closed her eyes as William's mouth moved across her neck. "Do I need to remind you about the priest and the immortal?"

He stopped and looked up. "Not if you want me to continue."

She gave a long, painful sigh. "Fine. How long will you need?"

"It depends."

"On?"

"How long you keep talking." William pulled his long black hair up away from her body and began kissing her once more.

Queen Pallanex reached down and grabbed a handful of his raven locks, pulling him up to face level.

William rose, his eyes were blood red and his teeth morphed into animalistic shape. "Is this what you want?"

"You know it is." She groaned in pleasure mixed with a fulfilling pain.

Their kiss was hard.

Afterward, William lay exhausted on his back. Queen Pallanex stroked his chest with her long thin fingers. A gold ring spiraled around the length of her index finger to a nail-sharp point. "Now can I see him?"

"No."

"I should command you." She rose up in frustration.

"And I should kill you."

"Hardly," she scoffed. "How much longer do I have to wait?

"I am almost finished."

"And then I can see him?" She turned her back to him.

"Possibly, when I get back." William tied the top of her dress for her.

"Such a gentleman…wait. Where are you taking him?" her curiosity spiked.

"With me."

"Why?"

"Do not worry. I can do both. I am very capable of doing two things at once." William gave a sly smile. "I will find the rebels in the south and finish my work with him."

"Good. When are you leaving?"

"That may take a while." William leaned into her close enough for her to see the tiny veins pulsate under his skin. "Because you wasted time letting those two useless bags of horse dung search for Marcus."

"Very well. When you return, we will discuss you being able to finally kill Marcus."

"Yes, I will destroy Marcus, the Heart, and the immortal. I promise."

"Good," she cooed. "That will open the door to my final plan. Are you sure you will be able to kill Marcus? I was always under the impression that you were afraid of him."

"What?" William roared. "I have never been afraid of him."

"Is it not true that when you were little boys you never fought him?"

"And he never fought me."

"You have had a chances to kill him."

"Those were not the right opportunities. I want a fair fight, me versus him."

I see," she said, not entirely convinced. She pulled her dress back over her tall, slender body. "Help a lady out." She turned her back to him.

William began to tie the straps back on, still leaving the bottom half of the dress ripped. "You could stay a little longer," he whispered in her ear as he pulled the cords tightly.

"No, darling, I have an army to gather…and you, my pet, have an army to raise."

"Give me what I need and I will kill them all…starting with Marcus."

"I believe you, my love. You have been loyal to me from the beginning, and you do your job very well. All of them," she purred. "I will see you soon." With that, she slinked to the door, down the staircase, and back to her awaiting carriage.

~ * ~

Once Queen Pallanex left his suite, William walked to the back of the room and poured a drink from a jug. "You miss those days? I hope we kept you entertained?"

A thin hairy leg moved out of sight from fear into the dark recess behind a pillar in a corner of the room.

"Do not worry. Soon, very soon, you will serve your purpose."

Chapter Five

Julie pulled her car into a spot designated for student drivers in the school parking lot. "Do you know how much cooler it is to be driving to school instead of riding a bus?" Julie asked Claire as they got out of her car.

"I can't believe your parents let you drive on the first day of school, especially your mom," Claire said as she straightened her skirt.

"I know, seriously. Thank goodness my dad was on my side." Julie hit the lock button on her key and the car beeped.

"Thanks for picking me up."

"Ah, Cedar Creek, how I've missed you," Julie said as she stared at the enormous three-story building and its glass atrium.

"You have?" Claire asked. "Didn't you just say…?"

"Yeah, that was weeks ago. I missed school."

"You are so confusing. I like school just enough to not have to do things for my mom around the house," Claire said.

"But look at this place," Julie said, looking around. "It's beautiful." She twirled around in complete happiness.

"What's wrong with you?"

"Okay, keep moving," the familiar voice of Mr. Frye urged. The school's principal smiled.

Julie smiled back. Mr. Frye, with his thick brown hair and mustache, was not the hard-nosed drill sergeant type principal everyone expected. He was actually warm and personable once you got to know him. Plus, Julie felt a little sorry for him knowing that Mr. Campbell used the Breath of Ostram on him to become a teacher in the school. A snarl almost formed before Claire interrupted. Julie shrugged. "I'm ready for a new school year. A new start."

The two walked across the marble tile, which spelled out "Welcome to Cedar Creek" in the center. "Good morning, Mr. Frye," Julie said waving at the school's principal.

"Good morning, Julie. Welcome back," he said, grinning. He patted down his mustache with his finger and thumb.

"I need all of you to make your way to the auditorium," Mr. Frye said.

"How do you do that?" Claire asked in a whisper as they walked past the principal and a succession of other teachers and administrators.

"Do what?"

"Don't act like you don't know," Claire said as they turned a corner to make their way to the auditorium.

"What?" They were handed brochures by a smiling Miss Slovarsky.

"You have this way of becoming every teacher and every parent's favorite person."

"I do not." They shuffled down the aisle and found three seats together by their cheerleading friends.

"Don't pretend like you don't know." Claire sat down. "Save a seat for Jimmy."

"Will do," Julie responded to the last question before answering, "I really have no idea…"

"Stop. My mom and dad love you. Mrs. Snyder loves you."

"The bus driver?"

"Yes. Always has. She probably cried today when you weren't there to be picked up."

"Stop!"

"Every teacher we've ever had. Mr. Campbell," Claire continued. Jimmy made his way toward the pair.

"Whatever."

"I'm serious."

"You're serious about what?" Jimmy asked. He sat in the saved seat and gave Claire a quick peck on the cheek. "Hi, Claire-bear."

Claire blushed.

"Nothing," Julie said with a sigh.

After the yearly greeting from Mr. Frye was over, the trio moved down the hall and waited in line for their schedules and locker assignments. "Good morning, ladies," a teacher said, breaking up their conversation. "Last name."

"Ayers."

"Here's your information," the lady said, handing her a piece of paper.

"Bennett," Claire replied.

"Here's yours. Have a great year," the teacher said in a rehearsed monotone voice.

"Thanks," Julie replied and smiled at the woman, who in turn smiled back.

"See?"

"See what?"

"That teacher likes you now."

"Oh, my gosh. You're outta your mind."

The two friends sat in the back of the auditorium for second-year orientation.

"So, basically we do and don't do the same things as last year except now we're sophomores and we don't get a tour of the building?" Julie commented on the proceedings.

"Seems simple enough."

They walked to their new lockers, which were only two away from each other. "I've got Spanish first, Mr. Vincent, again," Julie said.

"I've got French. Have fun with the Nazi."

"Yeah, thanks," she dragged out. "See you next period."

~ * ~

"How was Spanish?" Claire asked at the beginning of second period, chemistry.

Julie sat down at one of the high stools in front of the oversized desks. "I think you know the answer to that."

"You should have switched to French. Madame is the nicest."

"Yes, you should!" Jimmy interrupted. "What are we talking about?" He took a seat next to the two girls.

"We're talking about how Jules should drop Spanish and take French."

"I did this year. I couldn't take Señor Vincent another year," Jimmy confirmed.

"Good morning, class. Welcome to Intro to Chemistry." Their teacher was a skinny man with shaggy hair and glasses. He started the conversation with a brief introduction. "As you know, my name is Mr. Reynolds. Before we start, I want to ask you how many elements are on the periodic table."

Julie stared blankly ahead as a girl on the left side of the busy room answered, "One hundred eighteen."

"Correct. Now, how about naming a few that we're exposed to on a daily basis?"

"Gold," shouted one student.

"Ooh, a rich one," the teacher chuckled at his own joke.

"Oxygen," said another.

"Water," Jimmy answered.

"Um, water is not an element, Jimmy," Mr. Reynolds corrected. "It's a compound."

Jimmy slapped his forehead as the class laughed.

In the bantering commotion Julie decided to jump in with a response, "Iron!"

"Really? You're exposed to iron on a regular basis?" the shaggy-haired teacher asked with a condescending tone.

"Yeah," she shrugged.

"Okay then, I find that hard to believe, but let's get back to things that matter…get it…matter? A little chemistry joke there."

After the bell, Julie got as much teasing as Jimmy did. "Iron? How often do you hang around iron?" he asked.

She paused before replying. "I don't know. Isn't there iron in the kitchen?"

"Like a skillet?" Claire asked.

"Yep, see!"

"Does your mom even have an iron skillet?"

"I don't know," Julie laughed in embarrassment. "How about you?"

"What?" Jimmy smiled so wide it covered the width of his face.

"Water, seriously?"

"Shut up!" he laughed.

"It's a good thing you're cute," Claire said.

"I think that's my cue to leave." Julie waved at the hand-holding couple. *If they only knew.*

~ * ~

After fourth period, Julie walked into the bright pastel cafeteria. *Last year I started the year with a pizza and a salad. I'm not doing that again.* She selected her lunch and sat at the table with her friends.

"Okay, I love photography!" Claire exclaimed between bites of her tater tots.

"Why are you getting all of the cool classes?" Julie asked.

"What did you have?"

"Home Ec. Oops, I mean Family Living, or something like that," Julie answered.

"Why did you take that?"

"Cuz I thought it would be about eating," she joked before answering, "Not really, but it did sound more interesting. I'm just glad the classes are short today."

"They won't be tomorrow," her friend warned. "Hey, there's Mr. Campbell with Mr. Langston, Miss Slovarsky, and Schultz," she said, motioning toward the language arts teacher who was sitting with the other three teachers at their normal table. The same table Mr. Campbell, Miss Slovarsky, and Mr. Langston were sitting at last year when a fight erupted—Julie's first introduction to the man who changed her life. Correction, *ruined my life.*

"Miss Slovarsky is so pretty. I wish I had her hair," Claire pointed out the young teacher's long, jet black hair that reached to the middle of her back.

"And, of course, Mr. Langston is wearing a Buckeye shirt," Julie added, coming back to reality.

"Cool! I need to ask Mr. C. about helping me in the weight room," Jimmy said. "You wanna go over there with me?"

"Nah, I'm good," Julie answered.

"We've got him sixth period for mythology," Claire told her boyfriend as he headed to the table of teachers. Mr. Campbell was wearing a black suit coat over a white shirt and blue jeans. "I like that outfit on him."

"Yeah, I guess." Julie avoided making eye contact, but she saw him glance her way. She hadn't spoken to him since the day she went to his home to get him to stop the dreams, and even though she was still having odd, colorful whispers in her dreams, she wasn't ready to talk to him again.

~ * ~

"You blew off Mr. C's class!" Claire said loudly when she saw her best friend at her locker at the end of the day.

"No, I...went to guidance. I'm thinking about dropping his class, so I just sat in there the whole time," she answered.

"Why? It's probably the best class on the schedule."

"I just don't feel like—"

"Plus, it's Mr. C," Claire interrupted. "You know he'll make learning about ancient stuff cool."

"I don't know. I changed my mind. I want to try something else." She closed her locker and began to walk to the locker room.

Claire followed. "Like what?"

"I haven't decided yet."

"What's the deal?" Claire asked.

"About what?" Julie answered, knowing full well what she meant.

"You know what."

"Nothing, I'm fine. Why?"

"Well, last year, you would take any class Mr. C. taught, even if it was dirt digging. Now you don't want to take his class on something you think is cool. What gives?"

"First, there's no such thing as a class on digging dirt." Julie bobbed her head sarcastically.

"And what's the second?" Claire asked as the two started getting ready for cheer practice.

"I was just looking at my options. I had Mr. C. last year, and I'm not sure I can learn anything else from him."

"This class is different. Last year we were freshmen taking a boring class, and even then, he didn't make it boring. Besides, I thought you liked him."

"Um, gross." Julie scrunched up her face. The entered the locker room to change for cheer practice.

"Not like that. I mean as a teacher, though you did say he was kinda cute."

"Stop."

"I'm serious. Please don't drop the class. We'll have a blast."

"Let's go ladies!" the cheerleading advisor, a peppy looking blonde, demanded as they walked on to the track wearing shorts and t-shirts. "We've got two days before our first game."

"Great," Julie whispers. "Full blown overdrive."

"Why did we want to make varsity this year?"

"Just lucky, I guess." And they fell in with the other cheerleaders who were running around Mr. Langston's precious track.

"Are you going to myth tomorrow?"

"Dude, let it go. I don't know yet. I'm going to talk to guidance again."

"I think you should talk to Mr. C."

"Yeah, that's not happening. What would I say? 'Sorry, Mr. C. I think your class is boring so I'm dropping it'?"

"But it's not."

"You've been in there one day."

"And it was fun. And last year was fun."

Julie blew out a big puff of air. "We'll see."

~ * ~

"I can't believe you missed again," Claire said at the end of the following day as they met in the locker room before practice. "Today we broke into groups to research the major Greek deities."

"I told you I was going to guidance again."

"What did they say?"

"They gave me a couple options. I think I might take wood crafting."

Claire stopped and gave her a look. "Wood crafting? What? Why?"

Julie knew that she couldn't explain her way out of this. "I can learn to make things," she said weakly, raising an eyebrow hoping her friend didn't ask anymore.

"There is definitely something wrong with you. What did you do to my best friend?"

Julie grimaced. "I don't know what to do."

"Then talk to me. What is going on?"

"Nothing. I need to…to tell Mrs. Weber I might be late for practice."

"Oh-kay," Claire said slowly. "Can I ask…"

"Nope. I'll see you later." Julie gave her best friend a hug and bolted out of sight to her next class.

~ * ~

Just as Marcus was wrapping up a conversation with two students from his last period, he had a surprise visitor.

"Hey," Julie said as the last freshman student left his class. "I remember being like that."

"I would hope so. It was only last year." He stood to wipe his whiteboard clean. Marcus wanted to keep himself busy more than anything else.

"Yeah, I guess you're right. I was so worried in your class." Julie fidgeted and sat on a desktop.

"I didn't notice." He was wearing jeans, a blue striped dress shirt, and dark blue jacket.

"You barely knew my name at this point last year."

"I'm actually surprised that you could find my room. You've missed it two days in a row."

Julie swallowed hard. "That's why I'm here. I don't think it's a good idea for me to take this class."

Marcus circled around her, collecting books from the desks. "And why is that?"

"After everything that happened, I just don't feel like I should."

"I suppose you think this is funny?"

"What? No. Why?"

"Julie, this is not a game. I understand how mad you are and how upset you are. I told you last time we talked that I did…do. But you have to understand that there is something more important than you at stake."

"This is about me not taking your class." She hopped off the desk and stood in defiance.

"I wish it were. I don't care if you take my class or not. That's not the point. The good of Seras and the people of Seras is the point."

"Then why don't you do it?" she yelled, paused, and then repeated in a harsh whisper, "Then why don't you do it?"

"I can't. It's not my job. My job is to take you back to Seras." He moved away from her.

"Well, I hate to disappoint you." Julie began to walk toward the door.

"I doubt it."

"What?" Julie turned back to him. "Why are you being so mean?"

"Mean? I am not being mean. I'm being honest. Are you still having dreams?"

"Yes."

"See. You know I'm right." He rubbed his hands across his face.

"That doesn't prove anything." She crossed arms over her chest.

"Of course it does. There is something strong pulling you back, and you are taking it out on me."

"And you're taking it out on me!" she shouted.

"It's not my fault Callista died."

"Stop!"

"And if you don't go back, her death will be in vain."

"Oh, my God! Stop! Don't say that. It's your fault! You took me there to train with her."

"You're right. I did. But I did it because I wanted to make things easy for you. Besides, you liked her better."

"I still do," Julie said. She turned her back to him. "I couldn't trust…I can't trust you. You hurt people. You lied to me. You let Callista die!"

And there it was. She had finally told him everything that she had been harboring. Julie turned her back to him to hide her tear-filled eyes. Marcus moved closer to her. "She died knowing that you were going to save her world." He started to reach out to touch her, comfort her in some way.

"No! Stop! I hate you!" Julie ran out of the room.

"Well, that couldn't have gone any worse," Marcus mumbled to himself in the quiet of his room.

~ * ~

"Oh, my gosh! This is going to be the best day ever!" Julie screamed as she, Claire and three of her cheerleading friends raced through an amusement park. "This is amazing! Not a cloud in the sky."

"There's hardly anyone here," one of her friends noticed of the popular summer retreat.

"It's like we have the park all to ourselves."

"There are a lot of cute guys. Did you see those boys staring at you?" Claire said in a squealing voice, noticing the group of well-tanned boys with perfect smiles.

"No, they were looking at us."

"No, they were looking right at you," her best friend giggled.

"Let's play that basketball game," Julie said, twirling around, enjoying the attention she was getting.

"Step right up, step right up," a round older man with red hair bellowed from a booth. The game was simple. Shoot the basketball into the hoop three out of three times and win a prize.

Julie stepped up and eyeballed the game.

"Come on, little lady," the carnival worker said.

Julie was a little leery of the man who was wearing a brown sleeveless vest and no shirt, showing off his pale blotchy torso. She put a dollar on the counter and the man handed her one ball while placing the other two in front of her. "I can do this."

She shot the first ball, nothing but net. Julie bobbed her head, pleased with herself. The second ball hit the top of the orange square and banked in.

"One more," the game operator said, handing Julie the last ball with an eerie smile.

She dribbled twice, set her feet just like in practice rounds in her driveway or the school gym, and swish. The ball went in perfectly.

The other girls cheered loudly when the man handed Julie a large stuffed animal. "A penguin, my favorite," she squealed.

"Nicely done," the red-headed man congratulated her. The girls couldn't help noticing his stomach protruding from the vest he was wearing.

The carnival worker leaned in and said, "Come back soon, Julie."

She gave him a funny look, "How did you know my name?"

His wink creeped Julie out, and she hurried away from the game carrying her oversized penguin.

"How did he know my name?"

"Does it matter? He probably heard us yelling it," Claire answered.

The roaring sound of large metal wheels clinging for life to twisting rails caught Julie's attention. "Okay, we've got to ride that!" Julie said, pointing toward a monstrous roller coaster.

"I wonder how long the wait is," Claire asked. Normally, rides of that magnitude took two hours or more to get on; winding back and forth around the metal railing, making awkward eye contact with the same people over and over again.

But not on this day. The group strolled through the line without stopping. The ride attendant asked how many were in their party.

"Five."

"You'll need to go two, two and one. Go up to lanes one, two and three," the worker said in a cheery voice.

"You four ride together. I don't mind riding by myself," Julie said as they got closer to take their positions on the platform to board the ride.

"Are you sure?" one of the girls asked.

"Oh, yeah. It's no biggie."

"Then you should ride in the front," Claire suggested.

Julie shrugged. "Sounds good to me." With the sound of sharp hydraulic brakes, the next car came up to the loading area. Julie was ready to go solo in the front seat when she heard a boy's voice say he was a single passenger.

"Okay, you go to row one," the ride operator said.

She looked to see a cute, sandy-blond haired boy walking her way.

As they got seated and the shoulder restraints came down, Julie gave the boy a shy, crooked smile and then craned her neck back to see the faces of her best friends, all of who were feeling slightly jealous. She grinned ear-to-ear and winked at them. *This day is getting better and better.*

Julie held her hands in the air in anticipation as the ride began its long, cumbersome journey to the top of the hill. The car raced down the steep decline. Julie let out a few banshee screams as the ride rolled and spun its way through a dozen turns and loops. It was exhilarating.

"Whoo-hoo!" she yelled as the ride came to a stop. Everyone aboard applauded with satisfaction. Julie looked over to her newfound friend. "What in the world!" She was horrified to see that the person sitting beside her was not a cute tan teenage boy with blond hair, but the old portly red-headed carnival worker.

"It is time to come back to Seras," the man said warmly.

Julie screamed loud enough to wake herself up from her dream.

"I'm going to kill Mr. C.," she muttered in a tired state of anger, exhaustion, and annoyance. Julie hopped out of bed to get a drink of water from the bathroom. She could feel the change of carpet on her toes as she moved from her room to the hallway. Pushing the slightly closed bathroom door open, she stepped from the carpeted hallway expecting to feel the cool texture of tile. Instead, she found grass. Julie lifted her eyes and found herself in a jungle.

Oh, great. The sound of a waterfall multiplied the pressure she felt in her bladder. Julie walked further toward the rushing water. A bevy of shirtless men with their faces hidden and looking away were doing pushups, pull ups, and other body-building exercises. *What's going on?*

The thick green canopy of the jungle was dotted with sunbeams. In the distance, she heard the sounds of jungle cats and wild birds. The mist of the waterfall sprayed her face. Julie moved closer to the muscle-bound men to get a better look. Their bodies rippled. The sweat glistened off of their backs, shoulders, and arms. Julie beamed widely. "Okay, this isn't so bad."

Julie grazed her fingers across the back of one of the men doing pull ups. The man turned with a smile. It was the face of the old carnie worker from her last dream. "No!"

"Hello, my dearest Heart," the voice sung.

The other muscular specimens rotated to face her; all with the faces of the carnival worker.

"It is time to come back to Seras," all of the images said in unison.

Julie's expression quickly changed from pleasant to shock and anger. "Why!"

She woke up for the second time that night in a motion of fury; throwing her pillow on the floor and tossing her sheet back.

Her cell phone rang. Julie sat up and swung her legs over the side of her bed. "Hello," she answered. Her cell phone became an oversized beige rotary desk phone, complete with spiral cord and wall attachment line.

"Hello." The voice on the other end of the line was the carnival worker. He, too, was sitting on the edge of Julie's bed, right beside her. He was wearing brown pants and a dark vest. His portly stomach hung on his lap. He was talking on a black rotary phone.

Through the absurdity of talking to someone on the phone while sitting next to them, Julie quietly asked, "Why are you bothering me?"

"You have surprised me, Heart," the man began.

"Stop calling me that! Please, call me Julie."

"Very well, Julie," he responded.

"Who are you?" she requested cordially.

"My name is Redderick Bobo," he announced proudly. "But the real question, my dear, is why are you still here?"

"Well, Mr. Bobo, this is my home. This is where I belong," she replied. And then begged, "Why are you here?"

"I wanted to talk to you, and since you would not come to me, I decided to come to you and talk to you face to face," the stranger stated.

"Talk to me face to face over the phone," she smirked.

"This is your dream, my dear, not mine," Redderick added.

"So, if I wake up you'll be gone," she said, still talking through the phone.

"Eventually, but the only way to keep me gone for good is to come back to Seras," he informed her. "I would really like to meet you and the Solia Custor, too."

"The Solia who? Oh, yeah, Mar…Mr. Campbell," Julie figured out on her own.

"Yes, Marcus. He has been gone just as long as you have," Redderick explained with a chuckle.

"Sounds like your problem, not mine. Why aren't you haunting his dreams instead of mine?" the sleep deprived girl asked in protest.

"He is waiting for you to change your mind," Redderick said.

"Yeah, well, that's not happening," Julie continued her stubborn demeanor.

"I am afraid it is, Heart. You are trying to live in a fantasy world where nothing bad ever happens. That is not reality," he explained.

"Then what is reality?" she demanded, shifting her weight on the bed.

"This is reality," he said.

"No, this is a dream and Seras is a nightmare. It's not reality," Julie raised her voice.

"It is your reality, little girl—"

"No, it's your reality, not mine!" she interrupted loudly.

"You are more important to Seras and Earth. More than you will ever know," Redderick informed her.

"What does that mean?" Her anger continued to build.

"Come home to Seras and I will tell you," he prodded her.

"Seras is not my home!" she steamed, taking a swing at the portly old man with a pillow. The man evaporated into the night air. The pillow struck nothing, causing her to lose her balance and fall out of bed. She landed on the hard, carpeted floor with a thud.

Julie rubbed her eyes. It was daybreak—another sleepless night.

Chapter Six

The next morning, Julie pounded on Marcus Campbell's front door. She was ready to get this over with.

"Okay, let's go," she demanded as he opened the door. Her pace was quick as she headed for the basement.

"Good morning," Marcus said in a teasing manner.

"Yeah, yeah. I don't have time for pleasantries; good morning, Shakespeare," her growl softened to a purr.

Marcus laughed. "It's a good thing I have that cat, or you would have killed me by now."

"So are we going or what?" Julie insisted. Her hand was on the doorknob. He could see the impatience.

"Uh, what changed your mind?" he asked as he started to sit on the couch.

"No, no, no." She moved over to him. "There's no time for that," she said grabbing him by the arm lifting him back up from his seat.

"Just like that?" Marcus asked.

Julie tried with all of her might to get Marcus to move toward the basement stairs. "I haven't slept in forever. I'm tired of fighting him and I'm just tired. I'm going to meet him and then I'm going to punch him in the nose," Julie told him. "Why are you resisting so much?"

"Punch who?"

"Redderick Bobo!" she yelled.

The mention of the immortal human from Seras made Marcus pause. "Where did you hear his name?"

"I met him last night." Julie puffed out her cheeks. "I thought you sent him after me."

"He's here?" Marcus's voice sharpened.

"No, he's in my dreams. I told you," she stated in aggravation.

"What does he look like?"

"You don't know?"

"No, I don't know what he looks like. I've never seen him," he explained. "Remember, I once thought the stories of the immortals Redderick Bobo and Bhjuda Heilshorn were just that, stories."

"Well, they're not, and you aren't missing anything except that he is really annoying," Julie said as she continued her quest to get Mr. C. down to the basement and through the portal to Seras. "He's kinda old and round and gross looking."

"Oh," Marcus murmured in a relieved yet concerned tone. "What did he say?"

"I don't know," she answered, giving up trying to move him. "That he wants me to go back to Seras."

"Okay, wait a sec."

"What? I thought you'd be happy."

"I am. I'm just not ready. I'm not even dressed." Marcus directed her attention to his wardrobe of sweatpants and a sleeveless t-shirt.

"Like that even matters." Julie ignored his attempt to keep her waiting any longer. Then, while realizing she was gripping tightly to his arm, she noticed the size of his arm compared to her hands, and the muscular features of his frame peeking out from the low cut side of his shirt. For a split second, the thought of the possibility of the men's bodies in her dream being Marcus's…Mr. Campbell's. *Oh, yuck!* She shook off the thought.

"Fine," he relented. "Tell Shakespeare goodbye. He will pout if you don't."

Julie reached down, petted the happy cat, and followed Marcus to the basement door. They descended toward the dingy, gray basement and the scary red outline of a diagram. The diagram was a circle enclosing a number four and an inverted number four connected at the top to make a point. In some archaic way, it looked like an angel. It was those cursed markings that finally convinced Marcus that Julie was the person he was looking for on Earth. The number-like drawing was called the Mark of the Elders, and it closely resembled the number forty-four that Julie had worn ever since she was a little league soccer and basketball player. It was the only number she had ever worn—it was her favorite number. She couldn't help feeling nauseated about what it had done to her.

Once she got past the fear that her English teacher wasn't going to kill her in this creepy room, he whisked her away to another dimension: Seras. A place definitely stuck in medieval times. She met Callista and her friends, Otta and Seren, inarguably the most beautiful women she had ever seen. She and Callista trained constantly for at least four months, and she became the older sister Julie never had. Then she watched in horror and helplessness as a giant warlord killed Callista in the battle to protect the hidden village of Allon. Why was she the Heart? Why was she this chosen person? She didn't have any powers and she most certainly could not fight on a battlefield. Why is it important for her to return to Seras? She wondered. Then Julie stopped. She realized she had to return to face some immortal who kept disturbing her sleep and her life.

"Wait," she paused, straightening out her hand and pushing against Marcus's chest.

"You changed your mind?" he asked, stopping in confusion.

"Is this Bobo dude dangerous?"

"I don't think he wants to kill you, if that's what you're asking," he assured her. "But, I have never met him, and I have no idea what he wants."

"Great," Julie sighed.

"Do you still want to go?" he asked.

Julie knew he was hoping she said yes, but she was happy that he was willing to give her more time if needed. She let out a big breath of air. "Yes, let's get it over with."

They both watched as flames shot upward toward the ceiling but burned nothing. Julie felt Mr. Campbell's hand rest on her shoulder. While she was angry, Julie appreciated the attempt to comfort her as they stepped into the circle. He lit the purple lamp and snatched his hand back quickly. Time on Earth had just become irrelevant. She nervously closed her eyes and moved toward the angled center of the flames and disappeared in the light.

Julie found herself in the familiar position of portal travel. Even though it had been most of the summer since she last made the trip, the whipping wind on her naked body reminded her why she didn't miss the awkward feeling.

She felt Marcus release her hand. She knew he would grab his clothes, put them on, and leave the small dingy cabin he called home. Julie waited for the wooden door to slam closed. By now, the cold of the portal was normally replaced by the warmth of the non-air conditioned room, but not on this day. The cool wind sent a chill through her body as she shuffled as fast as she could toward the crude animal hooks where her clothes hung. Julie doubted anyone would walk in on her, but she refused to take any chances.

Julie ignored the extra layers of clothing hanging beside her normal outfit of brown deer hide pants and skimpy top tied with strands across her back. She sighed—another thing she forgot about over the last several weeks. Not only the idea of having deerskin hugging her own, but she was also still self-conscience of her young body. *"Baby fat," what an ugly phrase.*

"Why is it so flippin' cold in here?" Julie asked out loud in the empty room, rubbing her hands up and down her bare arms.

When she opened the door, she was met with a blast of frigid air. She had arrived in Allon. It was a charming place, and the brilliancy of the light made her think she was in some enchanted castle or fairy palace, for all looked like magic to her.

Marcus was standing next to Freya. He was wearing a thick black fur over his equally black frock, brown pants, and fur boots. Freya was dressed in similarly warm clothing, though hers were a great deal more colorful. They were both talking to the short, fat man from her dreams. They stopped their conversation and stared at Julie.

"Ah, finally, my child; let me have a look at you," Redderick gushed, his arms outstretched like a long lost relative.

Julie could not help but think that Redderick Bobo, the carnival worker from her dreams, looked like a cotton ball with his short stature and dressed in a pure white fur coat. She was amazed that she stood eye-to-eye with the immortal.

"Julie, you're going to freeze to death dressed like that," Marcus warned her, stopping Redderick from swooping in on his student.

"It's August," she protested.

"Not here." He escorted her back inside the cabin and helped her put on warm fur boots.

"Do I want to know?" Julie nodded in the direction of the boots.

"Bear."

"You could've just said no," she scolded him. "And the coat?"

"No," he responded with a smile.

Julie shook her head, narrowed her eyes, and pursed her lips.

"You told me to say 'no.'" He started to laugh, and then pulled back.

"What about the guy outside?"

"Redderick Bobo?"

"Yeah, him. Should I know anything about him?"

"I never thought he really existed." Marcus shrugged.

"That doesn't really help."

"I know. I wish I could help more. We'll just go with him, be polite, and listen to what he has to say."

"You're going with me, right?" she asked with a look of panic.

"Yes. I will not leave your side."

"Good."

Once she was properly dressed for the late fall weather, the two stepped back outside. Freya and Redderick were waiting along with a small crowd.

"My dear, look at you," Redderick started. "Tolth would have been so proud."

Julie gave him a doubting expression. "He wouldn't have been mad that I'm not some big, strong warrior?"

"No, no, no," the immortal laughed. "He knew all along you were going to be female."

"He did?" Julie and Marcus asked together.

"Oh, yes. If you could read the original translation, you would have known that," Redderick explained.

"Original translation?" Julie began.

"What is the original translation?" Marcus cut in. "I've heard that before, in the cave of Elderess Vestus. What does it mean?"

"That is a story for another day," the round immortal dismissed his request. "Now, if you will excuse us, this beautiful young lady and I have a lot of catching up to do."

Julie shot a frightened look at Marcus. "I'm not going anywhere with him!"

Marcus stepped forward to protect her.

"Now, now, now, please. I have been waiting patiently for the Heart to arrive," Redderick said. He wrapped her elbow in his and gently patted her arm as he began to walk away.

"Then I am coming with you," Marcus exclaimed. His sister gripped him by the arm to stop him.

"No, I am afraid that would be a horrible idea," Redderick said.

"She is in no danger, Marcus," Freya said, loud enough for Julie to hear. "And it is for her benefit as well as all of Seras that he talks to her…alone."

Julie tightened her lips in defiance. *Do I want to go with this guy who's been ruining my sleep or do I want to stay here with Mr. C.?* Her mind whirled. It was a lose-lose situation. "Fine," Julie finally said. "I'll go with you, as long as you promise to stop interfering with my sleep."

"Agreed," the short, chubby man said.

Marcus gave her a concerned look.

"Come, she is fine. Your men have been waiting for you." Freya guided Marcus from the front of his cabin and away from Julie and Redderick Bobo.

The immortal whisked Julie through the crowd, most of who reached out to touch both of them in reverence and to welcome Julie back to Allon. Julie continued to look back at Marcus. He only nodded to her in approval, though his face told a different story.

Redderick escorted Julie into his large, multicolored tent. She chuckled nervously to herself, thinking how fitting it was that she thought this immortal was a carnival worker and that he actually lived in a small circus tent. The room and walls were decorated in bright purple, blue, orange, and yellow colors with matching cushions on the floor.

The interior was warm. A small fire crackled from a stone hearth in the center of the room, the smoke of which drifted to a hole in the top of the tent. A pretty girl with long, thick, sandy-blonde hair was tending the flames. Five tall, well-built women, who Julie thought looked like supermodels, were lounging on the cushions lined up as long chairs and beds.

Redderick glared at the girl tending the fire. "Leave us, pig."

Julie looked at the short, bizarre man in disgust.

The one named Charlena stood to leave. Julie was astonished at the pretty girl's solid muscular build, undoubtedly formed from years of physical labor forced upon her at the hands of the immortal Bobo.

Then Redderick turned his attention to the women reclining around the room enjoying the warmth of the fire ring. "Ladies, I must ask you to give us some privacy," he said politely and apologetically.

The women looked at him in mild protest but then filed to the back of the large tent, not out of sight, but out of earshot of their adored guide and his special visitor. As the five passed the short, chubby man, they stopped to kiss him gingerly on the mouth. Warm bile rose in Julie's throat in revulsion.

Their movements were crisp and stiff. To Julie, each of them appeared spoiled and snooty, like beauty queens. *Why are they held in such high regard? They aren't any prettier than the girl he just called a pig.*

"I am sorry, ladies. I must insist." He held out both hands in an act of apology.

As soon as the tent was vacant of distractions, Redderick turned his attention to Julie. "Come, come, my dear. Have a seat." The immortal plopped down on a large cushion and patted another cushion facing him.

"I think I'll stand," she folded her arms a crossed her chest in protest.

He laughed a quirky laugh. "As you wish, but you and I have a lot to discuss. You will have to learn to trust me."

"Trust you? I don't even like you," she said flatly, not holding back her feelings. "Give me a reason I shouldn't punch you in the face?"

He frowned. "That will change in time. I am here to answer all of your questions…," he stopped short.

"All of my questions?" Julie asked doubtfully before relenting and sitting down. "Good! Then tell me why you have me here and why you insist on killing my sleep?"

"Very well," he turned serious. "You are here so that I can teach you everything you need to know about Seras, and how you came to be the Heart."

"It's about time!" Julie squirmed in her seat to get comfortable for the story.

"Yes it is," he said. "I apologize for, as you said, 'killing your sleep,' but it was important for me to get you here and start as soon as possible. The quicker I finish, the quicker you can fulfill your duty." He patted her on the knee.

His touch made Julie feel queasy after watching him make out with the five women and knowing he could enter her dreams. She was beginning to regret taking a seat. "Then, let's get started," she said, flinching away from him.

"First," Redderick said, apparently noticing her disdain, "I need to give you something." He got up and pulled a cloak out from a trunk. "This is yours," the immortal handed her the soft hide wrap. "I hope this makes peace between us."

"Why would it? What did..." she started. "Why did you have it?"

"To get you here. I can do amazing things with an article of clothing, a clear mind, and a little motivation," he winked.

The feeling of lukewarm liquid returned in Julie's throat at the thought of what he was suggesting. "Okay, can we get started now?"

"Today, I would like us to get to know each other," Redderick said. "Then tomorrow I can start the story of Seras."

"Tomorrow? Um, I'm not going to be here tomorrow."

"Of course you are," he said, taken back by her comment.

"No, after this little chat I'm going home."

"But my dear, you are the Heart of Tolth, the protector and defender of Seras." He appeared confused by her statement. "This is your home."

"I hate to be the one to break the news to ya, but this isn't my home and I don't live here."

"I do not understand."

She faced him and talked real slow, hoping the words would sink in. "I am here because you were messing with my sleep. I do not want to be here. I am done with this place. So tell me everything you think I need to know so I can leave."

"But, my dear, my story is much too long to tell you in one sitting."

Julie stood. "That's okay. I really don't want to hear any of your pathetic little stories."

"Oh, this is no mere story, child. This is the greatest story ever told throughout Seras. This is also your story and how you came to be."

That caught her attention, but she stayed defiant. "How I came to be is easy. I know the birds and the bees, and how babies are made."

"That may be so, but let me guess: you have an unsolved mystery concerning your birth, do you not?" he asked with a glint in his eyes.

Julie knew she was stuck. Her mother would kill her if she didn't find out why Julie was the first Ayers girl born in generations. "Fine. Tell me one of your stupid little stories." She sat back down.

He laughed. "And tell me, dear, just what are stories anyway? They have to come from somewhere. Somebody had to think they were worth sharing and take the time to tell them."

"You mean make them up." Julie spoke with a certain amount of hostility.

The immortal laughed. "Little girl, stories such as these are not make believe."

"How do I know this whole thing isn't just some long, crazy dream?"

"And what if it were? Is there anything wrong with life intermixed with imagination and dreams?"

"It's not real."

"Ah, to the dreamer, the storyteller, they are very real. Those dreams can spring to life in a creation all of their own. Say a poor farm boy is forbidden from ever being with a certain pretty girl, so the lad watches her from afar. Day after day, night after night, soon the lovesick fool envisions the trees in the woods as beasts and the hedges surrounding her house are castle walls. His story unfolds in his quest to rescue her and prove his undying love. It does not make it false or wrong. It is the way he sees it."

"What's the point?" she sneered.

"The point, my dear, is that every story has a reason. The reason you and I are here was written long before we existed. The stories are there to be told. For if they are not, they fade away like yesterday's sunset, never to be seen again. And that is why I am here—to keep the sunsets alive now and forever. Without the knowledge of why you are here and what came before you, you will never hope in understanding what is needed to be done."

"You sound like Mr. Langston."

"Who?"

"My history teacher," she started to explain before saying, "...never mind."

"This is why I must insist that you stay here with me so that I can tell you everything you need to know."

"That's not going to happen. Here's the deal. I have school, cheerleading practice, homework, friends, and not to mention my parents that I need to see every day, so I will promise you that I will come back to Seras and listen to your stories, if…" Then she repeated the last word louder to make sure he got the point. "If, you stay out of my head. No more weirdo dreams. No more hazy chants. No more nothing. Deal?"

Redderick Bobo looked at her. His face contorted with confusion and mixed emotions. Julie could tell he was not used to be spoken to in this manner, and he was someone who always got what he wanted. But if she was the Heart of Tolth, there must be power in the title because he slowly said, "I do not know what to say."

"Say 'deal' and we can agree to me visiting often and you can tell me your stories without screwing with my head."

The immortal smiled slyly. "Deal."

~ * ~

Marcus looked around at the transformation the fortified city had undertaken in his extended absence. The exterior walls had changed from wooden posts to thick stone blocks. The old wooden ramps to the second level were now supported by thick white stone. The interior remained the same with the only exception being the old dirt paths that was once used as crossroads were now paved with small, white pebbles. "You've done good work since I've been gone," Marcus said to his sister.

"We have been busy. The Battle of Yellow Fields woke us up as to how close danger to Allon was," she responded.

"The Battle of Yellow Fields," Marcus whispered. His voice faded. Truth be told, he wasn't sure how he was going to react to going back to Seras knowing the happy face of Callista, the first person to forgive him, would no longer be there.

Freya must have sensed that when she said, "We kept the fortress there, rebuilt it as an outpost. We named it The Callistan Tower. Argos, his sons, the Hemoor women and others spent a great deal of time preparing it."

"She would have liked that." A soft, melancholy smile formed on his lips. "Have there been any other attacks?"

"Attacks?" Freya asked, confused.

"Don't play dumb. You have had attacks inside and outside of Allon. Have there been any more occurrences?"

"No, brother, everything is good. We are perfectly capable of handling problems without you." The two continued to stroll around the walls. "Griffus and Pertheus have been in charge of construction and fortifying the city."

"They have done excellent work." Marcus stopped and gave a puzzled look. "Where's Jayna?"

Freya tilted her head slightly. "She is away on a scouting mission. I needed her in Cauleta. She is safe."

"That is not what—" A commotion drew his attention away from Freya. Julie appeared in a huff. Marcus watched her stomping her way toward him. "This can't be good," Marcus said. He swiftly met up with her. "What happened? What did he do?" Marcus was extremely wary about the immortal's intentions.

"Nothing! He told me some B.S. about storytelling and promised to explain why I'm here." Julie stopped. "Sorry, I didn't mean to say 'B.S.' to you."

"That's okay, I'm just confused," Marcus said, scratching the back of his head.

"You're confused? How the heck do you think I feel? First, he wanted, no, insisted that I stay here forever. Like that's ever going to happen. Then he tells me he knows my whole family history and that I need to know everything so I can do my duty."

"I'm—"

"Forget it. Get me out of here." She stormed past him and Freya to Marcus's cabin.

Marcus didn't feel like he had much of a choice. He chased after her and helped get her back to Earth through the portal. Once there, they followed their procedure of him keeping his eyes closed as she gathered her clothes and went up the basement stairs. He dressed quickly but not fast enough as he heard his front door slam before he made it upstairs.

Chapter Seven

"There." William pointed to a wooden stronghold on the other side of the River Linsay. "Not quite the fortress Artavious once fought under." He joked more to himself than to the men under his command. The fortress looked ragged and barren. None of them were with him when he and Marcus once laid siege to King Artavious and his men of Hawkmir. The once beautiful towers and gardens now lay dead. A pitiful wasteland of rot and decay. The kingdom of Hawkmir immediately southwest of Cauleta was the last to lay between the Skorei and the Evandells. William gripped his black handled sword, forged in the womb of Evandell. In fact, he looked at the faces of his army and spoke aloud, "Most of you probably have never heard of Artavious the Bold. That is because we wiped out his kind before the lot of you could hold a sword."

"My lord," a gruff faced man sputtered, "why did we travel here? This is not worth our time."

"I would agree with you," William said. "Except I never asked for your opinion." His threatening look sent the man back to his unit. William thought about killing the questioner, but he thought the man would more than likely die soon enough for William's little task. He had traveled southwest from Cauleta to the River Linsay and the lands of the Hawkmir to find the so-called rebellion Pallanex was concerned about. "I hope they have enough men to make this worth my time."

In the distance, William could make out the presence of a large mountain lion perched on a rock at the edge of a thick wooded tree line high above the impending fray. *Waiting for dinner or an obstacle to fight?*

Hawkmir men began to form on the far side of the riverbank. They stayed far enough away that William could not make out their faces or size them up in any way. Obviously, they had spotted William and his men on the other side of the water. They fired a barrage of arrows toward him. As he watched men fall around him, William thought about how he should have traveled across the narrow water during the night fall to avoid their disadvantage right now. They would have to cross the murky water while warding off the bombardment of Hawkmir bowmen.

"Move!" He ordered as men scurried around avoiding the death from above. "Get across the river!" He plunged into the cold water. Light rippled from the water's surface. His men followed. William knew if he could get across the water before too many arrows caught up with him, he would be able to buy his men time to get across.

The Hawkmir men resisted the urge to advance. They chose to continue their long range attack. An arrow pierced William's arm. He winced in mild pain as the tip sunk into his shoulder. He moved through the chest high water stroking with one arm as he tried to pluck the shaft from his shoulder. Blood pooled around his black uniform.

The body of one his men floated beside him. The pale face of death stared at him.

William made it to the other side. He crawled across the surface of the unwelcoming flatland. He was met by the release of hounds. Large black dogs with blade sharp teeth. One snarled and sprang toward him, gnashing at his skin. He grabbed the dog by the throat and tossed it into another menacing beast.

If he was not so angry, he would have been impressed by how the Hawkmir prepared to defend their pathetic land.

He was finally able to stand to his full height. The hounds were ripping his men to shreds as the ones who made it across the river came to shore. William helped his men free themselves from the jaws and claws of the large dogs. Killing all of the fine beasts in the process.

William stood corrected, Pallanex did have a reason to be worried in the south. Though, he did notice the continuous volley arrows had stopped. *Have they run out?*

Before enough of his men had gathered, the charging sound of men and horses came crashing down on William and those that had made it. The Hawkmir soldiers were shabbily dressed. They had little or no armor. Their clothes were tattered and patched together. Their swords were old, some even carried rusted armor and swords. Those that wore helmets were made from bone of wild animals.

William rubbed the spot where he was struck by an arrow. The bleeding had stopped, and healing had begun.

William drew his sword and met the Hawkmir defenders as they swooped in on him and his men. He cut down men and horse alike. The seemingly overwhelming odds against him spurred him to enjoy it even more. In a small lapse from commotion he laughed and began morphing into the Skorei beast. His skull began to jut out from his nose and jaw; his long sharp teeth extended from the canines and the lateral incisors from both the top and bottom position of his mouth much like the death hounds he had just killed moments before. A ribbed "V" formed across the bridge of his eyebrows and surrounded his temporal bone. William's entire body structure began to expand; muscles rippled from under his black garments, and thick claws protruded from his hands.

His men caught a second wind from their leader's transformation. The Hawkmir warriors retreated back to regroup. Victory for William would soon be at hand.

He led his men to the Hawkmir gates. The men and women on the frontline were even more ragged with thin bare clothes, wielding the shell and horns of the black lodears. Bowmen sprouted out from atop the castle ruins. More of his men fell to the ground.

"By the Blood of Urvasus!" William shouted as he swung his blade at an attacker, striking the man full across the chest nearly ripping him in two. "What in the name of Azahleah's Beast are you doing?" His question was directed to one of his soldiers who had turned to retreat from an onslaught of enemy fighters.

"My lord!" the coward yelled as he drew nearer. "Help me!"

William muttered incoherently, stepped in front of the horde and grinned. The men paused for a quick moment in time then gathered the courage to advance. William battled his way through the throng. Killing five of the men before more of his soldiers closed around him. The skirmish was going well except for the lapse of the one who started to flee.

He and his men broke through the lines and into the ancient ruins of the once proud kingdom. A small swarm of smartly dressed warriors met beneath a decayed wooden archway embedded in crumbled buttresses. They had come from hiding near a retaining wall. The last of trained warriors from Artavious's reign met William whose eyes were as red as fire, fangs bared, ready for carnage.

It had been too long since William had enjoyed the primordial screams of dying men. "Kill them all!" he ordered.

The battle came to a close. He walked through the old ruins, perplexed. He found the soldier who had tried to flee from the fight. "Come here, boy."

The man shrunk as he approached his commander.

"Have you ever heard the saying, 'Live well. Die well'?"

"Y-y-yes sir," the man stuttered.

"Good, how about the old Skorei saying, 'No one lives'?"

"Y-y-y-yes sir. That was a battle cry for yourself and M—"

"Do not say his name," William yelled. The man cowered in fear. "Do you remember another saying from the one we shall not say his name?"

"Yes, sir, 'Show no mercy'."

"Good. You are an educated man in the ways of the past."

"Yes, my lord." The man refused to look up or make eye contact with William. He clearly feared for his life.

"Look at me," William commanded.

The man obeyed. His breath caught in his throat and he began to shake.

He lifted a hand to the man's chin to steady his shivering head. They held each other's gaze. "Ah, there it is," William said in a low, pleasant tone. "Have you ever noticed the seductive reflection in a person's eyes at the precise moment they realize that there is no escape from death?"

William moved his hand from the man's chin to his neck. He slowly crushed the man's throat with his hand as blood slowly seeped from the coward's nose, mouth, and eyes. He discarded the lifeless body then turned to a nearby soldier. "You!"

"My lord," one of the men asked.

"Would you like to tell me where all of the women and children are?"

"Sir?"

"The women and children," he said again, waiting for the soldier to understand. "Have you ever been to a city where there are no women or children?" He walked to the gate of the ruined fortress.

"No, my lord," the man answered. The hair on his arms stood on end, and he began to breathe more shallow.

"Precisely," William snarled. He looked to the precipice where the cougar once laid in waiting, now no longer there. "So tell me where they are!"

Chapter Eight

Julie watched Redderick Bobo carefully as he sat down on the pillows beside her. She moved away from him, not allowing him to get too close. "I'm here, just like I promised." Julie hated the idea of coming back to Seras, but she promised the immortal that she would. Her return to Mr. Campbell's house a few days later surprised him, but he agreed to escort her back. *I guess I should be nicer to him,* she considered to herself. *But not yet.*

"So you are. You are a woman of your word. Tolth would be pleased about that."

"Are you sure? He wouldn't be disappointed that I'm just a girl?"

The man laughed. "Oh, my dear!" he exclaimed. "He always knew you would be a girl." Then he wiped a tear from his eyes.

"I'm glad I could amuse you," she said, a little confused and a little frustrated. She poked a stick into the fire pit. "Everyone else seemed disappointed that I was just a girl." The smoke rose and it reminded her of an evening roasting marshmallows and making s'mores. "If only," she whispered.

"I am sorry, but you see, the only reason people did not know you were going to be female is because they did not study the prophecy as closely as they should. It is very clear."

"But Marcus, Freya…everyone?"

"None are as wise as they think they are. Some even choose to ignore what they already know." He beamed and then patted his knees with his hands. It made a loud clap. "Now, where would you like me to begin?"

"Well, I think it only makes sense to start from the beginning," she requested.

"Wise girl, very wise indeed. The beginning is a very good place to start."

Lyrics from *The Sound of Music* raced through her mind and brought a smile to her face. "So you can tell me the entire story from start to finish, and why I am here?" she asked trying to avoid eye contact with his grotesque belly button that seemed to be peering at her.

"Ah, time…You see, I can tell you the start, I can tell you why you are here, but only you can write the ending."

"I don't understand."

"You will, my dear, you will. Now let me begin…"

In the time before man, angels were here. Their purpose was and always has been to worship their Father, creator of all. There are different orders and different rankings of the heavenly hosts, but that is not important now. For the story is of the five angels who became the ones we now call The Elders.

"The Elders were angels?" Julie interrupted.

"Indeed, you see my dear girl, I am many things, but most importantly, I am the recorder of time and events for the world we know as Seras."

"A history teacher."

"If you insist, a history teacher. I will tell you all you need to know if you only take the time to listen."

"I will," she agreed, taking the hint that he didn't like being interrupted.

"Good," the pudgy little man responded with a nod. "First, you must know that angels have the essence of either male or female. Tolth, Ostram, and Azahleah each take the form of a male. Eryx and Vestus both take the appearance of females."

"Okay," Julie drew out, not sure why the information was necessary to the story.

"This is what happened," Redderick Bobo continued.

The time had come for the angels to assemble in the great hall. It was a marvelous room, immaculate with white and gold as far as the eye could see. The glory of heaven lit up the universe with a spectacle never witnessed by man. A canopy of celestial stars emerged high above the vestibules. The floor shimmered of silver and gold, and the palace walls glistened with the brilliance of diamonds. This was the realm of God.

All of the angels had congregated by order of the archangels; well, almost all of the angels.

In flumes of smoke and light that held the secrets of the true forms of the winged creatures with multiple eyes and tails the angels, Tolth, Ostram, Vestus, Azahleah, and Eryx, appeared so they, too, could join the holy army as they were told of their mission.

The archangel, Michael, emerged before the gathered forces of Heaven to tell them the news. They must strike down one of their own, Lucifer, the Morning Star, God's most beloved angel.

"Lucifer has set himself above Our Father's plans. He has gathered a following of Cherubims and the archangels Beelzebub, Belial, and Samael to follow him," Michael solemnly informed them.

Many were surprised when they heard about the plan to strike Lucifer from Heaven. Tolth collected himself near the commander of the archangels, Michael. "Is it true, Michael, we must condemn Lucifer to the abyss?" Tolth asked with grave seriousness.

"It is true," the chief archangel responded gravely.

Eryx was stunned. "Lucifer is our brother, she protested. "We have to fight our brothers and sisters?"

"It is Lucifer's choice. He is the one being disobedient to our Father. The others are only following his foolish decision, so they must be cast away too," the general of the heavenly host spoke with authority.

66

"Where are the Seraphim?" Tolth inquired of their stoic leader.

"The Seraphs will not be joining us, neither will Azrael," Michael *answered.*

"We will need Azrael!" Ostram stated loudly.

"Wait, who is he?" Julie cut in.

"Azrael? He is an archangel – a very powerful archangel. The great Angel of Death," he answered. "Now, where was I? Ah, 'they needed Azrael'."

The archangel, Gabriel, joined the conversation, "It is time." His words silenced the conversation between Michael, Tolth, and Eryx.

The angels collected around Michael and Gabriel to listen to the final instructions. The archangel, Gabriel, was to lead Zachariah, Tolth, Eryx, Vestus, Ostram, and Azahleah along with two legions of celestial warriors into battle as the first wave of the attack against Lucifer's forces. The archangels, Michael and Raphael, were to lead the final legion, including Zechariah, Uriel, Castiel, and Azariah.

"Wait! I've heard of Michael, Gabriel, and Raphael. They're in the Bible," Julie interrupted again.

"I am sure you have. They are the most loyal and respected of all the angels in Heaven. May I continue?" he asked.

"Oh, yeah, I'm sorry." Julie shifted in embarrassment.

In the instant of a blinding light, the mighty Gabriel, manifested in the more recognizable form of a man, stood before his brother, Lucifer, and those he had convinced to join him in this act of treason. When the angel Abdiel saw the anger in Gabriel's eyes, Abdiel vanished from Lucifer's side to beg forgiveness from his Father. The legion of angels appeared behind Gabriel. Lucifer and his legion stood firm in their presence.

"The time for warnings is over; quit this unwise rebellion, my brothers and sisters," Gabriel commanded.

"They are with me, my brother," Lucifer taunted. "We stand together no more. Join me and we can set things right. The way it should be." His voice was proud and ominous.

A tear of sadness fell from Eryx's eye.

Gabriel drew his sword and moved closer to Lucifer. The angels from both sides unsheathed their weapons and began to advance toward one another. Heaven rang out from the clanging of swords and the yelling of the divine champions.

"This is when the devil was banished to Hell?" Julie interrupted yet again.

"Yes, this is when Lucifer was banished from Heaven into the pits of Hell," the ancient storyteller explained.

The commanders of Lucifer's mutinous angels, the archangels, Beelzebub and Belial, and Azazel, a cherubim loyal to Lucifer, led a group to flank the attacking host. The Battle of Heaven was long and costly.

The angels Mammon and Moloch were the first to fall. Their piercing screams echoed loudly as they were expelled from the heavenly realm.

Uriel and Castiel attacked their sister, Mulciber, quickly overwhelming her.

Gabriel fought his way toward Lucifer. The heroic Tolth led Eryx, Ostram, Vestus, and Azahleah to stop Beelzebub, Belial, and Azazel's movement to conquer their leader. The five angels, we now know as the Elders, clashed with the two archangels, Azazel their former brother, and many other of the defiant ones.

Michael appeared with his legion and they, too, began to fight against the rebelling angels. Countless angels on both sides were injured and killed.

Lord Tolth swung his sword recklessly in every direction, fighting off the advancing legion. Ostram and Azahleah were both knocked down and nearly killed by Belial. Eryx blocked the forthcoming blow, allowing Ostram and Azahleah to regroup. Eryx, Ostram, and Azahleah battled the former archangel to the point of defeat, sending the commander of Lucifier to hell.

"Okay, wait. I have two questions. Can angels be killed? And, why haven't I ever heard of Tolth, Eryx, and the others you are talking about?" the curious girl again stopped his story.

"Yes, angels can be killed, but only by other angels." He held up his hand to stop her from asking another question. "As for your other questions, I will get to them, my dear. I am just now getting to the good part." He smiled and began again.

Vestus with all of her might and glory fought with Azazel, striking the angel down with a fierce swing of her sword. Tolth cornered Beelzebub and the two clashed to near exhaustion. Beelzebub lunged forward to strike Tolth down, but Tolth swiftly moved and wounded the powerful archangel. The momentary loss of reaction from the traitorous archangel allowed Tolth to finish Beelzebub, causing Beelzebub to vanish from the hallowed battlefield.

By this time, Gabriel and Michael had made their way to Samael and Lucifer. The great archangel Gabriel defeated his archangel brother Samael in a battle of honor and power.

Finally, with a mighty thrust of his sword, Michael dispatched Lucifer to the abyss below. His cry could be heard roaring throughout the universe. A heavy toll was paid for the fallen angel's insubordinate ways; they had all been banished from Heaven into the fiery abyss you call Hell.

The immortal finished his story. Julie sat for a moment gathering her thoughts.

"Okay," Julie broke her momentary silence. "What does this all have to do with me?"

"That was the beginning of Seras," he said.

"You didn't say anything about Seras, only the five so-called angels," she smirked.

"Ah, but that was only the beginning. You see, after the battle to condemn Lucifer and his army of followers to Hell, their Father was pleased with their actions. He named them the Five Lions of God. Their almighty Father gave the five the power to be custodians of this world hidden from Earth's dimension," Bobo said with a twinkle in his eyes.

"Why them?" Julie asked.

"The others continued to serve and worship their Father in Heaven and continue their work on Earth," he told her. "It was probably their first mistake," he said sadly.

"What do you mean?" The comment left Julie curious for more. "I have a lot of questions."

He laughed. "I am certain you do, but as for now, I have other things to do, and I am sure Marcus is chomping to get you back to your home," he said.

"Are you kidding me?" Julie exclaimed.

"I have much more to tell, but we have plenty of time, dear girl," he continued.

"I thought I needed to know this crap so I could help you destroy some kinda evil something," she stammered.

"You do, you will, but all in good time." Redderick stood and offered her a hand to get up from her cushion. "This is why I wanted you to stay in Seras."

"No, thank you," she said, brushing his hand away and standing on her own.

"Please, I insist on you letting me take you back to Marcus," he suggested.

"No, thank you, again," she answered. "I can find my way back, thank you very much."

"Very well." He clapped his hands twice and Charlena entered from outside in the cold. "Give her her cloak and wrap and make sure she gets back to the Solia Custor safely," he demanded.

The girl nodded and did as she was told. She escorted Julie toward the tent door.

"Wait," she paused. Charlena and Redderick stopped. "The Solia Custor, Mr. Campbell, is he my teacher, my mentor, or what?"

"Yes," he responded.

"Yes? Yes, what?" she asked.

"Yes, is yes, my dear. I will see you again soon," he dismissed her. The frustrating immortal clapped three times and his harem scurried to him as fast as their feet could take them.

Julie left with the sandy blonde servant, Charlena, as quickly as possible before the warm liquid bile began to escape her mouth.

Chapter Nine

"Here we go!" Julie yelled. She was sitting on Claire's shoulders, holding up the top corner of a large banner.

The band started playing the Cedar Creek Penguin's fight song.

She hopped down and sprinted with the other cheerleaders across the field as the football players crashed through the paper banner. Each girl had their hair pulled back with green and yellow ribbons.

The home crowd roared in excitement. It was the first home game of the season. Everyone had forgotten about last season's lackluster record. A new year, a new hope.

"This is so much better than last year," Julie shouted to her best friend.

Claire smiled in agreement. Last season, they were junior varsity cheerleaders and only cheered once on a Friday night. That homecoming game was the same game where Julie first saw Mr. Campbell's eyes light up during a lightning flash. *I still have no idea why that happened. Being a warrior from another dimension wouldn't do that, would it?*

Julie picked up one of the large flags and ran back and forth in front of the stadium.

"If you can run that fast carrying a giant flag, you can run fast enough to be on my team."

It was Mr. Langston. He was always trying to get Julie to come out for track, and she liked the extra attention.

"Okay, ladies," the cheer advisor shouted over the band. "Time for the Welcome Cheer."

The girls lined up and waited for the senior captains to give the command before going into their routine. This was followed by a dance they had practiced all summer.

The fans clapped loudly.

After the band played the school's fight song one more time, the crowd focused on the flag being raised by local retired military men and women as the band played the national anthem.

Claire waved to Mr. Campbell as he walked by the fence.

Julie just nodded.

"Are you two cool, again?" Claire asked.

"Eh," Julie shrugged. "I wouldn't say cool, but we're getting there."

"Well, I'm glad."

~ * ~

The next morning the familiar knock on his door told Marcus that Julie was ready for her trip to Seras.

"Are you ready to go?" Her demeanor toward him was still lukewarm.

"I am if you are." Marcus smiled. He opened the basement door. "How did we do last night?" He motioned to let the girl go down first.

"You didn't stay for the whole game?"

"No, I had papers to grade."

Julie got to the bottom of the steps. "Well, you didn't miss much. We lost."

"That's too bad," he said, lighting the symbol on the basement floor. The flame grew and spread across every line.

"Why? You don't even know anything about football."

73

"True, but I have kids in my class who play for the team and cheer for the team." He winked.

"Oh."

They stepped into the circle. Marcus lit the candle that slowed time on Earth during their absence, and they walked toward the bright center.

She grabbed his hand to brace herself for the travel. This was her first true sign of letting him back into her good graces. When the swirling wind came to a stop, she let go of his hand. Marcus stepped out first, grabbed his clothes, put them on, and walked out the door to wait for Julie to catch up to him.

Freya approached the two. "I am afraid he is not here."

"Where is he?" Marcus asked. Julie walked out and looked around.

"I have learned not to ask questions," Freya answered.

"Well, great, I guess we can go back," Julie said.

"We could stay and get some work done," Marcus suggested.

Julie didn't look thrilled. "Okay, I guess…wait, can I go find Otta and Seren first? I haven't seen them in like forever."

"Yes, that would be fine. I will meet you back here when you are ready."

"Cool!" She took off running down the road toward her Hemoor friends.

"Is that wise?" Freya asked.

"What can it hurt?" he answered, turning back to face his sister.

"You are just gaining her trust again."

"It's a false trust. We both know it," Marcus adjusted his coat in the cool air.

"Then why risk it?"

"Because I want her to be happy. Is there anything wrong with that? She spends all of her time here with Redderick, learning who knows what…" Freya gave him a puzzled look. "I worry about her.

What if he is doing something to her? What if he is manipulating her somehow?"

"You care about her."

"Of course I do. I wish she wasn't here. I wish there was a different way."

"But there is only one way," Freya said.

"That's what we've been told." The two walked around the fortress. "So where is he?"

"I told you, I do not know," Freya answered.

"I find that hard to believe…"

Their conversation was interrupted by Pertheus. "Freya. Marcus, it is great to have you back."

"Is there a problem?" Freya asked.

"No, I was wondering if you, Marcus, and the Heart were going to be here long?"

"I am leaving that up to her. She went to see Otta and Seren. I think it's best that she decides."

"Well, as long as she is busy, would you care to join us for a meal?"

"I would."

The three, Marcus, Freya and Pertheus, met with Griffus, Argos, their wives, Argos's three sons, Julius, Jakob and Edwin at a building toward the center of the village. Tables and chairs lined the perimeter. A large cask of ale sat in one corner. A band of musicians played happy music.

"It has been a while since we have all been together like this," Griffus said. He moved slowly across the room from getting a drink, the residue of his injury still affecting his mobility.

"Much too long," Marcus said. "What's the word from Cauleta?" He looked at Argos. "Have you heard from Jayna?" He was worried about the Tarrack girl. While he was glad their relationship had healed since the time they first met, there was still a hint of guilt of what he and his type had done to her people. *Those feelings will always be with me.* And those feelings could be extended to most of the people in the room.

Griffus stopped Argos before he could answer. "There is no word, but let us not talk business. Let us talk about pleasure."

Marcus got the hint. They needed a break from the day-to-day stresses of their lives. He could escape to Earth and get away from it, but his friends were stuck here. "My apologies, but it appears you have been having a bit too much pleasure as it is." He shifted his head toward Laila, Griffus's wife, a dark blonde woman who was very pregnant.

"Aye, that I have."

"It is no pleasure carrying this much weight," Laila sneered playfully.

"Well, I am a hardy man. There must be a hardy son in there." Griffus laughed.

"Or daughter," Laila countered. The rest of the crowd laughed along with the couple.

"Tolth help you if you have a daughter," Argos joked.

"No, help the poor boy who tries to court her," Gwendolyn added.

"That is the truth," Laila agreed. The two women moved to a table, where the experienced mother of three, Gwendolyn, started giving advice to the mother-to-be.

Pertheus handed Marcus a drink. "Thank you."

The girl named Leyta walked into the room with another woman. Edwin got up and met the tall, dark-haired beauty right away. He took her to an open seat next to him.

The air between the two brothers was frigid. Argos and Gwendolyn looked at each other. Marcus could see sadness and concern in their eyes. Even the oldest brother, Julius, had a look of disappointment.

When Julie, Otta, and Seren walked through the door, a sense of relief overcame Marcus. The excitement level of the room increased at the arrival of the Heart.

Jakob stood and clasped Otto by the arm. He escorted her to the center of the floor and twirled her around to the sound of the music.

Pertheus, Jakob's commander, stood and took the new girl by the hand. She was small with light auburn hair and giggled at the attention from Pertheus. "I cannot let a fellow soldier dance alone," he said.

Seren quickly joined the dance party, fastening her hand to Otta and Jakob's, spinning and twisting across the floor with laughter that broke any tension.

Julie practically hopped over to Marcus. "You didn't tell me you were going to a bar."

"I think I'm the one that should be worried. Are you old enough to be here?"

"Ha! Haven't you heard? I'm the Heart of Tolth. Apparently I have no rules," Julie said and bobbed her head in playful defiance.

"Funny, very funny," Marcus responded.

Pertheus brought the auburn haired girl to Marcus and Julie. "Marcus, Julie," the commander started, "I would like you to meet Erayna."

The woman curtsied. "It is a great honor," Erayna said. "I am a descendent of Evandell, Alanas's sister."

"It is my honor to meet you. Your sister was a very brave warrior." Marcus stood, held the girl by her shoulders, and kissed her forehead.

"As I hope to be someday." She bowed her head in honor.

"I'm sure you will," he replied.

Julie hopped out of her seat awkwardly. "It is my pleasure to meet you." She looked at Marcus and kissed Erayna's forehead, too.

"Thank you," the girl said, backing away.

"Okay, that was weird," Julie said. "Why did we do that?"

"I did it because her sister was killed in a battle trying to defend me. I don't know why you did it."

"I did it because I thought I was supposed to. Oh gosh! She probably thinks I'm nuts."

"Well…" he teased.

"Stop." She rammed him with her shoulder. "That poor girl. I can't imagine."

"No, it's…" Marcus paused. He watched the people on the dance floor. They were having fun, even though there was tension between Jakob and Edwin, even though evil was out there ready to strike, even though death was certain for them before their time, they were laughing, dancing and enjoying these moments of happiness. "Come on." He held out his hand.

She gave him a surprised look. "Okay."

He led her to the dance floor and they clapped and danced along with the rest of the crowd.

~ * ~

Heart, oh Heart, time to wake up.

The voice sounded familiar to Julie. She awoke with a start. It was Redderick Bobo. "You told me that you were never going to sneak into my dreams again!" she yelled.

"I did no such thing," the immortal said.

Julie wiped the sleep out of her eyes. It had been the first peaceful sleep she'd had in months. First, it was the irritating dreams from the weird little man she now knew as Redderick Bobo; then it was her pangs of sadness from still being mad at Mr. Campbell. Now Redderick was back. "Yes, you did. You promised!"

The man laughed, further angering her. "My dear, it is morning and you are in Seras."

"What?"

"You must have had quite an evening," he chuckled as he handed her her boots. "Come, we have work to do."

She looked under her blanket. *Thank goodness*, she thought as she saw the draping of cloth covering her body. She still waited for him to turn his back to her before sliding the covers off, sitting up on the bed, and pulling the furry boots over her feet.

"Where were you?" She stood and straightened her clothes.

"Here, you will need this too." He handed her the cloak that was hanging on the rack of deer antlers.

"Thank you, but that doesn't answer my question."

"I was busy making preparations," Redderick said, opening the door and stepping outside. "Come now, we are running late."

"Your fault; not mine."

"Very well, if you must know. I deliberately stepped away for a few days to gather my thoughts and make my peace with the Elders." He hurried down the street with Julie practically chasing after him.

"The Elders are gone."

"Ah, that is where you are wrong." He turned to her and said in a hushed voice, "You see, only Ostram is completely gone." He spun back around and continued his way to his tent.

Julie jogged to catch up. "Whoa, wait. Now I'm confused."

"Don't be confused," he said. "But I am getting ahead of myself."

"Hold on a minute. You just made a conjunction? Now I'm really confused." Julie followed him into the tent. The women were lounging on the pillows. The one named Charlena was tending the fire to keep them warm.

"I apologize. I am a master of languages. I picked up on your speech pattern quickly. Such an ugly way to speak."

"I think it's more convenient, and you are changing the subject."

"So I am." His smile reminded her of a rattlesnake.

"Master," the women cooed.

He motioned them away. "Hello, yes, hello," he said as they took turns kissing him in adoration. "Yes, yes, please, ladies, I must ask you to leave us."

The women scurried about and left the tent. "You too, cow," he commanded Charlena.

"Why are you so mean to her?" Julie demanded, not being able to take it anymore.

Redderick looked offended. "She is a slave. She is my slave to do and say as I please."

"Why?"

He grew hard and his voice changed. "That is none of your business. Your business is to listen to what I tell you."

The girl left the two.

Julie gave him a cold stare. "I think we're done for the day."

Chapter Ten

As the first half of school came to an end, Julie was happy with the progress she and Mr. Campbell had made. Their relationship had improved greatly from the beginning of the year when she didn't want to be in his presence at school or on Seras. The one class she had him for, mythology, the class Claire had to convince her to attend, had become her favorite by far.

"Hey, what do you think about Johnny Appleseed?" Claire interrupted her thoughts about Redderick Bobo and the way he treated the slave girl.

"I don't know; he seems too clean cut," Julie answered, looking at the fresh-faced boy from their chemistry class.

"Well, duh. That's why we gave him the name."

"Gave who what name?" Jimmy asked as he sat down beside them.

"Um, nothing."

"Yeah, right."

"Okay," Julie confessed quietly so the teacher didn't hear. "We started giving guys nicknames so nobody knows who we're talking about."

"Really, like what?"

"We have Johnny Appleseed, Paul Bunyan, John Henry…"

"Those are guys from Mr. C's folktale lessons," Jimmy said.

"Yep," Julie answered. In class, Mr. Campbell offered up popular folktales and tall tales and other stories of heroic adventures or how things came about in the minds of people from days long ago. Those lessons built the groundwork for the rest of the semester's lessons, ideas, and assignments. "We use other myth heroes too."

"Like whom?" he asked.

"Gilgamesh and Enkidu," Julie answered.

"Enkidu," Jimmy giggled with a snort.

"Hercules..." Claire added.

"Or Heracles, depending on who you ask," Julie corrected, using the famous hero's Greek name over his Roman name.

"I think you should ask 'you know who' out."

"I think you're nuts," Julie answered.

"Why? First of all he's cute, smart, funny, and second…third…or whatever he's really into you," Claire responded.

"How 'bout we call him Apollo?" Julie didn't wait for Claire's sign of approval. "Because he looks like a sun worshiper with his blond hair and tan."

"Wait, wait, who is that?" Jimmy laughed.

"We can't tell," Julie squealed.

"You can tell me."

"No way," Julie said.

"I'll tell you later." Claire nudged him playfully.

Julie opened her eyes wide for fear of Jimmy finding out who she thought was cute.

"You guys are such nerds."

"Myth nerds," the two said in unison.

"Thank you very much," Julie finished.

"Girls are so weird, man."

~ * ~

Inside a large circular stone amphitheater set with five thrones rising above the dais, our five angels – the Five Lions of God – the Khamsah Aryad Ilalo – settled into the role of guardians of their new world. They gathered to discuss important matters. The arena was decorated with the flowers and fauna of the world they no longer considered their home.

"Why did you gather us, Tolth?" asked the raven-haired Vestus. Her dark skin glistened from the light of the sun. She was the last to arrive. She stood tall and magnificent in the arched doorway.

"Tolth did not summon you. I did," Eryx said abruptly. She moved from the five rock thrones to a position in the center of the dais. A circle lit with brilliance.

Tolth followed quietly. He took a spot across from Eryx and a line was formed inside the circle that connected the placing of the two elders.

"Very well," murmured Ostram. He got up from one of the royal seats and stood in the circle. Another line formed below him.

Vestus and Azahleah did the same. The Elders' Symbol formed under their feet and surrounded them. A swirling wind enveloped them, yet inside all was calm.

"May I ask now why we are here?" Vestus asked in a tranquil voice.

"We need to name this place," Eryx answered.

"Did we need all of the spectacle?" Ostram asked, bowing his head slightly in a sign of respect.

"This will bind our words, for we have many important things to discuss," Eryx said.

"You said we needed to name this world," Tolth said. He did not like being surprised.

"That is our first order of business," Eryx answered. She brushed her hair off of her shoulder.

"Then let us begin," Ostram said with a smile.

Azahleah chuckled before he threw out the words, "Aestius, Aatone, Morthys, Pymbra..."

"Ah, the old language. How I have missed it," Ostram mused.

"Stop! Those are all too morbid," Vestus bellowed.

"Vestus, I am surprised at you," Ostram said.

"Fire, chasm, death, or shadow? Those are your ideas for a name of a place so beautiful?" Vestus criticized.

"Seras?" Tolth suggested.

"Seras...beauty?" Eryx paused. "I like that."

"As do I," Ostram agreed.

"And I," Vestus approved with an acknowledging smile.

They waited for Azahleah. "Very well, Seras it is."

"Good, that is settled," Eryx said.

The others nodded in agreement, satisfied with what they had done.

"Now I suggest we create servants for us," Eryx said in the whirling wind.

"I do not understand," Tolth said.

"Why do we need servants?" Azahleah asked, his eyes wild with distrust.

"We need someone to do our bidding," Eryx explained. "We need a warrior to handle any necessary problems that may arise."

"A warrior? What problems are going to arise, sister?" Tolth asked.

"I believe she is right," Vestus added before Tolth got his answer. "A warrior, a male warrior would be useful."

Ostram and Tolth looked at each other. Azahleah stayed away from the debate. He figured his opinion would be ignored.

"Then let it be done," Ostram said.

Tolth nodded. "I would like to add a second servant. A recorder of time."

"For what purpose?" Eryx asked.

"To journal the history of what has come and what will come."

"Very well, you can have your servant to keep history."

The five placed their hands together. A beam of light appeared in the middle. The form of a man appeared. He was dark skinned, tall, and muscular. They named him Bhjuda Heilshorn, which translated to 'immortal man of the sword.'

"Whoa…is that why he has two names?" Julie asked, stopping his story.

"It is," Redderick answered.

"How 'bout your name?"

"I was just getting to that."

"Sorry." Julie shrunk, knowing her interruptions infuriated him.

The Elders kept their hands interlocked and a second human appeared.

"Much more handsome than the first," he interjected.

Julie sucked in air to keep from laughing or rolling her eyes. While she had never met Bhjuda Heilshorn, she believed everyone was better looking than Redderick.

"They named me Redderick Bobo, which translates to 'he who records time'."

"Oh," Julie uttered. "Now it makes sense. So they aren't really first and last names, they're your translated name."

The immortal nodded in agreement. "We were born from the light of the Elders and we are marked with the Elders' Symbol." He showed the emblazoned sign on the upper part of his shoulder blade.

Great, an image I'll never get out of my head, Julie thought, closing her eyes and shaking her head vigorously.

"Once the Elders had created us they moved on to other matters."

"On to other topics," Eryx proposed. The swirling wind came to an end, but they held fast inside the circle at her words.

"What is left?" Ostram asked.

The raven-haired Eryx answered, "We need to divide up the realms."

"I do not understand," Vestus said. "Why not continue to manage this world as before?"

"This world, Seras," Eryx said, using its newly given name for the first time, "is not going to thrive as Earth does if we continue to get in each other's way."

"What are you saying?" Azahleah asked in a defensive tone.

"Eryx is right," Tolth stepped up to Eryx's defense. "Seras will be better served of each of us takes control over different realms."

"I take it you have a plan?" Ostram asked Eryx.

"I do."

"Then let us hear it," Ostram prodded.

"The five realms are water, sky, land, man, and spirit. Each of us picks a realm that suits our taste. You will protect it, nurture it, and it will flourish."

"How do you suggest that we decide, Eryx?" Tolth asked.

"Yes, sister, how will we decide?" Vestus asked with a hint of trepidation.

"I suppose we discuss it," Eryx answered.

"And if two or more want the same realm?" Ostram continued to inquire about the details of the proposal.

"It goes to a vote," Eryx replied.

"Do we all agree?" Tolth wanted to confirm before moving forward.

One by one, the five agreed to the terms. Eryx was first. She was obvious in her excitement to be in control over one particular realm.

"Which do we divide first?" Vestus asked.

"That which is most important," Eryx said in a tone that suggested her intent.

Tolth remained the voice of reason. "They are all equally important."

"That is not necessarily true. What if we all want to control the realm of man?" Eryx snapped.

Her purpose was now apparent.

"Perhaps, some do," Ostram spoke out. "I, however, would like the realm of water."

"The other four looked at him with mild surprise. Ostram was quite possibly the wisest of them all, and for him to not want man was indeed smart of him," Redderick Bobo stopped to make the commentary to his story.

"Why?" Julie asked.

"You shall see."

"Very well," Tolth agreed. "Is there an objection?"

None came.

"I will take the spirit realm," Azahleah said. "If that is to your agreement."

"It is," Tolth said.

"Yes," Vestus agreed.

"I do not object," Ostram nodded.

"Then so be it," Eryx exclaimed.

"He wanted the underworld?" Julie paused.

"He did. Azahleah had always had a taste for the morose."

"If I can, may I have the air realm?" Vestus asked, knowing Eryx would not protest.

"Is there any objection?" Tolth asked Eryx.

"No," she pulsated.

"Then it is up to me and you, sister. Which would you prefer?"

"I am sure you want man as much as I do," Eryx said.

"No, I would be happy to control the land realm," he answered.

"Why?"

"There is no need for us to make this difficult. I will take the land; you may have man. Everyone will be happy."

"You are positive?" Eryx asked a final time.

"I am." Tolth smiled.

"Very well. Thank you, my brother."

"Is there any more business we need to discuss?" Ostram inquired.

"No," Eryx answered happily.

"Then there is work to be done," Ostram spoke with a quiet authority.

"Agreed," Tolth said. The small congregation began to disperse from the auditorium.

"Wait!" Eryx commanded. "As a show of good faith, I would like for each of you to consider creating new life."

"Do you think this is wise?"

"I do."

"Create what you wish. Let us make Seras a place different from Earth."

"Very well," Ostram said. "I can manage that."

The others agreed and took leave of their sister.

"A place better *than Earth," she said once alone.*

Redderick spoke directly to Julie, "Ostram was the first to try out his new power."

Lord Ostram wisped through the wind in a long train of white smoke to a meadow near a raging river. The riverbank was swollen like a pregnant woman spilling out from its banks across plush grass reaching to the tips of the hanging willow trees. Being sensible, Ostram knew he had to use his power wisely.

Before he could start, his brother, Tolth, streamed into the area in a cloud similar to his own and materialized beside Ostram. He noticed the sad expression on Tolth's face.

"Tolth, you look pained," Ostram said offering a hand to his brother.

"I am. I know I sounded certain that I could do this, but I may be wrong." He faced the shorter Ostram with determination.

"There is a first for everything," Ostram joked.

"How do I begin to take on such an undertaking? I am not God. It is not my place."

"No, it is not. But are we trying to be God?" He motioned his hand at the meadow and the clear stream. The colors were vibrant and alive.

"We cannot do this. God gave us this place to care for and maintain," Tolth argued.

"Unfortunately, I believe Eryx is right. He would want us to branch out and take possession of this and make it our own."

"Have you tried, yet?"

"No." Ostram saw the look his brother was giving him. "I was going to get ideas from you."

Tolth saw past the deceit.

"Being the admirer I am of feminine beauty on Earth, I thought I would design a race of water nymphs to keep me company." He grinned, knowing that his response would irk his brother.

"You cannot do such a thing!" Tolth protested.

"I can," Ostram defended lightly.

"Where is the honor?"

"There is plenty of honor in making our own creations."

"How so?" Tolth questioned.

"What you create with your own hands is a tribute to the gifts given to you by our Father. If done with the right frame of mind, the thought of honoring him by using your talents is His greatest wish."

"Then why haven't you?"

"I told you. I came here to get ideas from you."

"Why lie?"

"What makes you certain that I am lying?" Ostram stared deep into his brother's eye. "Tolth, are you concerned that my choices will not be admirable."

"This does not feel right to me."

"I promise I will not make beautiful women who fawn over me and serve my every need." Ostram gave a wicked grin.

"Why play games with me?"

"Because it is fun. Do not worry. Whatever I create will be useful and honorable to all."

"Thank you, my brother." In another wisp of white smoke, Tolth was gone.

This left Ostram to his own accord. Then he designed his perfect creation. He went to a place of solitude away from the meadow and into the quietness of the deep swamps. He bent down and scooped up a handful of mud. Ostram whispered into the nighttime air words long forgotten in this world or yours. He breathed a mouthful of wind into his hand and threw the clump of mud into the swamp. The scattered fragments of dirt and water rose up. They looked like three-foot tall furry frogs. Ostram named them Greagons. Then he ordered the first one to speak. And he named him Ter-Ra.

"Why 'Greagons'?" Julie interrupted.

"The Greagons look like tall furry frogs that can walk and talk like humans."

"That's not what I meant and not what I've heard." Julie chuckled, thinking how she had heard them described them as if a cat and frog mated and stood upright.

"Greagons were perfect to Ostram because they were scavengers and non-threatening to his brothers or sisters. They viewed the small creatures with sympathy. And because of their diminutive size and lack of physical beauty, none of the other Elders cared much for them nor desired their worship."

"Mr. C…Marcus told me about him spending time with the Greagons. They sound funny. I hope I get a chance to see one."

~ * ~

The next morning, Marcus and Julie were off by themselves outside the gated walls of Allon. He was wearing brown deerskin pants and a brown sleeveless shirt. Julie was wearing a similar deerskin pants and a top crisscrossed in the back. They began a light exhibition of wooden swordplay.

They tapped gently and moved slowly at first.

"It seems like forever since I've done this," Julie started.

"You've been pretty busy," Marcus agreed.

"I know. Basketball and homework are killing me," she said as she moved back and forth, blocking his easy two-handed swings.

"I was talking more about your story times with Redderick," Marcus said, delving for an explanation without asking outright. He changed thoughts when Julie spun away from one of his jabs. "Don't turn your back on your opponent."

"But it seemed cool." She smiled.

"Only at this speed. In a real fight, you wouldn't make it all the way around." He looked down, forcing a look of disapproving eyes.

"Okay." Julie crunched her face.

"I thought he disgusted you." Marcus continued in his curiosity.

"Oh, he does. He's really gross, but I have to admit, the story of the five angels defeating the devil was pretty cool," Julie said. She eluded his attack by jumping on a stone precipice. When Marcus moved closer to swipe away her feet, Julie launched herself over his head with a no-hand cartwheel and landed behind him.

"That was nifty." Marcus blocked her backhanded swing by thrusting his sword behind him quickly.

"Mr. C., nobody says 'nifty' anymore," Julie shook her head at his "uncool" nature.

"If you would've thrust instead of swung you would have got me," he coached.

"I'm not going to jab you in the back!" she said in an insulted voice.

"Julie, you have to do whatever it takes to win."

The little trainee made a noise with her lips in protest. "Fine."

"So, what else has he told you?" Marcus asked as they picked up the speed of their exercise.

"I don't know. It's hard to overlook the grossness of his bare belly sticking out past his vest or whatever. Then you have the disgusting way his harem girls treat him like he's the world's greatest lover," she mockingly shivered. "And, then I loathe…yeah, that's a good word for it…I hate the way he treats the other girl, Charlena."

"That's why I was curious. It doesn't sound like you like being around him, but you keep going back to hear his stories." They moved into the woods, where she ran from tree to tree avoiding his attacks.

"Well, he tells stories a lot better than you," she giggled, hiding behind one tree, running swiftly to another and another before Marcus could spot her.

"Like?" he asked, thinking he had cornered her but seeing nothing behind the tree.

She held her breath trying not to give away her position. Marcus lifted his head and caught her scent in the air. He moved silently through the twigs and leaves. In one motion, he leaped onto an overhead branch ten feet directly above her.

Julie's curiosity got the best of her and she tried peeking around the tree to find her teacher. When she didn't see him or hear him, she left her spot and moved back to the tree she had been hiding behind before. Marcus dropped quietly behind her and followed her step for step.

"Looking for me?" he taunted.

Julie screamed. "Holy crap! How did you do that?"

"Always keep your eyes busy. Look everywhere," he instructed.

"You didn't tell me you could fly." She hit him with her sword.

"Ow! I can't fly."

"Then where did you come from?"

"Hey, you did a little trick, I did a little trick. It's all fair," he said, rubbing his arm.

"Seriously?"

"I can jump really high sometimes," Marcus half explained.

"How high?"

"I don't know; I've never measured it," he said.

"That's cheating," Julie protested.

"How is that cheating?"

"You didn't tell me you could jump over my head," she pouted.

"Well, you aren't very tall," he joked.

"Hey!" She batted him with her sword again.

"Are you ready to go again?" He laughed, rubbing the mark the crude weapon left.

"Yep," Julie snorted as she hunched down and gripped her sword with both hands.

Marcus spun his wooden blade confidently. "I have to say, at least you take getting beat well."

"Hahaha. If you didn't cheat, I would've kicked your butt," she responded, whacking her sword against his.

"Not going to happen." At this, Marcus showed off a little, using his sword to guide her weapon to the ground and then swiftly scooping it up with a reverse grip, trapping her sword between his arm and side. She was disarmed and staring at the width of his blade.

"Well, not if you keep doing fancy crap like that." She didn't give him the satisfaction of acting impressed. Julie picked up her weapon and reset herself for battle. "So, who taught you how to sword fight?"

"My father was the first, and then I had a trainer," he answered remorsefully. First, thinking of his father, then the thought that he had played a role in both Canis and Kralen's deaths.

"Why the face?" the attentive girl asked.

"What? Nothing. I haven't thought about my father in quite a while."

"Redderick told me your dad was a great warrior," she said, hoping to make him feel better.

"Hmm. What else has he told you?"

"Not much about your dad; that was the only thing. He always leaves me before he answers all of my questions," she replied.

Marcus took a breath and calmly restated his previous question. "What else has he told you? Heck, you probably know more about Seras than I do."

"I doubt that." But her pride swelled, just as Marcus had hoped. "They have been mostly stories of the five Elders. I guess they used to be called the "Five Lions of God.""

"Hmm?"

"Oh, yeah, they helped defeat the devil and send him and his demons to hell. Then, as a reward he gave them the power to rule this…planet or whatever it is."

"See, you do know more about Seras than I do." Marcus continued to stroke her ego, which got the youngster talking even more.

"Did you know Seras is a word meaning "beauty" in some kind of language?" The bubbly brunette was a fountain of information. "I guess it's some angelic word or something."

Marcus only had to smile and nod, the sword training was over for now, but he was learning everything he needed to know about the crafty immortal's teachings.

"There used to be a large gateway between Earth and Seras so they could share common…stuff." Julie paused. "I know 'stuff' isn't a good word, but it's the best I can come up with."

"What kind of stuff?"

"Sometimes people and animals would wonder across the gateway without realizing they had left Earth. Then they started building villages and raising families. That's how Seras started," Julie said with a smile.

Marcus smiled back at her. That simple acknowledgement allowed Julie to tell him more.

"But," she said in a high-pitched voice, "God knew that it was taking too long for Seras to be completely inhabited, so He granted them the power to create life forms and help populate Seras even more. Procreating was taking too long," she giggled. Marcus gave her a stern look. "Oh, don't get all professorly on me," she protested before continuing. "Redderick told me these powers would also help the five establish lordship over any problems that may occur." Julie sat down on a smooth patch of grass. Training was definitely over for the day. She was busy talking, and Marcus was more than happy to listen.

"So what did the other Elders do?

"I don't know, yet. Redderick said 'Ah, we will get to that, child'," she said mocking the pretentious speech of the immortal. "He says that a lot. I wonder how old I'll be by the time he tells me the whole story."

This caused Marcus to laugh aloud. "It sounds like you are learning a lot from Redderick," Marcus said honestly. "I didn't know about all of that."

"How do you not know all of this stuff?"

"I never really thought about it. When I was growing up, there weren't history classes or…or any other classes. All we did was learn how to fight. Most of the people picked an Elder to worship and worshiped him or her. We didn't know how the world got started; we didn't care how the world got started. We cared about living and dying." Marcus purposely left out the fact that he probably killed anyone who actually knew the history of Seras.

"So, I'm basically the teacher here," she proudly joked.

"I guess you are."

Chapter Eleven

"So, the Greagons saved you, right?" Julie asked Mr. Campbell a few days later in the weight room. They started their workout sessions shortly after football season was over, her duties as a cheerleader were finished, and her goal of making the basketball team for the winter began.

"Yes, why?" he looked around, hoping no one heard her say the word 'Greagon.'

"Oh please, Mr. C., nobody is paying attention to us." They looked around at the self-absorbed student body. "See. Anyway, Redderick was telling me the story of Ostram and that he created them. But his reason was kind of confusing."

"How so?"

"He told me that the only reason he created them was so that the other Elders wouldn't want them to worship them. How does that make sense?"

"Ostram had his reasons. I get that he didn't want the others to take away his creation or fight over their adoration."

"I don't get it."

"Imagine if the other Elders thought that Greagons were somehow attractive or useful. Then they would want the Greagons to worship them instead of Ostram. Jealousy is an ugly thing, and power is worse."

"Yeah, I guess you're right."

"Of course I am." Mr. Campbell smiled.

In many ways, Julie was glad to have him back on her side. She still didn't like the idea of fighting, killing, dying, or anything else that went with it. But she knew she needed Mr. Campbell to be there for her. And there was one final thing to put their past behind them…well, two actually, but she could not think about the second thing right now. "Hey! After we're finished here, how would you like to come over for dinner?"

"I would love to. Is it okay with your parents?"

"Of course it is." Julie smiled.

"Are you sure?"

She glared at him.

"Okay," he relented.

"Yay!" She hopped up and down, clapping her hands excitedly.

~ * ~

Marcus was relieved that he was once again navigating the gravel road that led to Julie's house—something he hadn't done since the sad night in the rain following Callista's death.

The blue two-story house stood lit up with decorative lights wrapped around the white railing on the front porch. He parked in front of the two-car garage underneath Julie's basketball hoop.

As Marcus walked up the porch stairs, he couldn't help laugh that the family even decorated the small swing with green garland. He opened the screen and knocked on the door.

Julie opened it as if she were waiting for him to arrive. "It's about time."

"I'm five minutes early."

"Whatever. We've already started without you."

Marcus stopped to think about what she just said. "I must've misund—"

"Oh, Mr. C, you are way too easy. I was just kidding. Get in here."

He could only shake his head.

Julie's father, Phillip, met him in the hallway and took his jacket. "Hello, how have you been?"

The two men shook hands.

"I've been well. Thank you."

"It seems like forever since we've had dinner together."

"Yes, much too long."

"I think since before we left for London," Michelle said, meeting him just in front of the kitchen entryway, wiping her hands on a towel.

Marcus reached his hand out to shake hers, but she moved past it and gave him a hug.

"It is so good to see you again. We tried to get Julie to call you over the summer."

Julie gave a panicked look.

"I know, she did," he lied. "I was out of town most of the time…visiting my sister."

"Oh, she should've told us."

"You know how teenagers are," Marcus joked. Julie's brown eyes expressed gratitude for covering for her, yet he knew he would hear about the crack he just made about teenagers.

Not much had changed since his last visit. The Ayers' home was cozy with the same patterns of blue and brown in the living room. The wooden banister was covered in tinseled wreaths.

"I decorated the tree all by myself," Julie bragged, showing off their Christmas tree that was lit up and fully adorned. The smell of pine and wassail filled the air.

The family sat at the kitchen table with one member missing.

"Patrick is at a concert," Julie said.

"I see."

"Julie, it's much better than that," Michelle said. "He is part of McPherson's men's ensemble."

"It's a Christmas choir with all guys," Julie explained. Probably thinking he didn't understand.

"I think it is quite an honor," Michelle said.

"I think it's kinda nerdy," Julie added.

"Don't be rude, young lady."

Julie scrunched up her face and sat down at the table.

"Please have a seat," Phillip said, pulling out a chair for him.

"I hope you like chicken," Michelle said.

"I do," he responded. He was a little surprised they served him something other than meatloaf.

As far as Marcus was concerned, Mrs. Ayers was the best cook he had ever known. She had the table overflowing with food: meatloaf, salad, macaroni and cheese, steamed broccoli, and rolls with butter.

Julie and her family bowed their heads and Marcus followed in kind.

"So how is your sister?" Michelle asked after Julie's prayer.

"My sister is doing well."

"Now where does she live again?" Mr. Ayers asked.

"She lives pretty far from here."

"Dad, why don't you tell Mr. C. about what you did to your car," Julie said. Marcus could tell she was trying to change the subject.

"What did you do?" he feigned interest and played along with Julie's distraction.

Julie's father began a long and elaborate one-sided conversation about the work he put into his baby, the 1976 metallic blue Chevy Nova. The car that almost hit him when he entered Earth for the first time.

The meal was as delicious as always. The conversation ranged from Phillip's car to school and basketball.

Michelle then brought up her favorite topic, "Did Julie tell you what we discovered on our trip?"

"No? It must have slipped her mind."

"Oh, it did," Julie frowned.

"Well, while we were there, we found information about a young soldier, Duncan Ayre, except it was spelled A-y-r-e. He was part of something called the Royal Highlanders and fought against the colonists. Isn't that incredible?"

"I think so," Marcus answered with a little bit of confusion.

"No, not the part about fighting the colonists, but that we finally made the connection between our family and a family 'across the pond,' as they say." She used her best British/Scottish accent to say 'across the pond.'

Julie pinched the upper bridge of her nose with her thumb and forefinger in shame.

"I think that is fascinating," he said.

"I knew you would, being a history buff and all."

"Mom, he teaches English."

"I know, but he also teaches mythology, and that is history at the highest level, in my book," Michelle said.

After dinner, Julie and her family escorted their guest to the door.

"Thanks for coming," Julie said.

"Yes," Phillip Ayers said, sticking out his hand.

"It has been too long."

"Hopefully, next time won't be as long."

"I agree. I don't think there is anything keeping me away now," Marcus said, secretly referring to Julie's anger at him and shunning him for the entire summer.

"Maybe we can catch one of Julie's games together."

"That sounds like a good idea."

"Thank you for everything you do for her. I know she thinks the world of you," Michelle mentioned, handing him his coat.

"Thank you. It's really no problem. She's just a minor pain," he started.

"Hey!" Julie protested, brushing a strand of hair behind her ear.

"I was just kidding."

"I know."

"Well, you are welcome to come back for dinner anytime you want." Michelle smiled.

"Thank you."

"Can I walk Mr. C. to his car?" Julie asked her mother.

"Sure."

The two walked down the front porch steps. "Thank you again for coming over," Julie said.

"Of course, it was my pleasure," Marcus responded.

"And thanks for covering for me about this summer."

"Well, what was I supposed to say?" he asked with a wink.

"Yeah, I guess you have a point. And I did save you from having to try to explain where your sister lives."

"Very true." They stopped at his driver's side door.

"But, you did have to listen to my dad talk about his car and my mom talk about ancestry stuff," Julie said with a laugh.

"That's okay. I find them both interesting."

"I find it annoying."

"So, when are we going back?" Julie asked.

"We can wait until after the holidays."

"Seriously?"

"Yes, you love this time of year. You have basketball practice and we have plenty of time."

"What are you going to do?" she asked.

Marcus stopped and looked at her.

"What?" Julie asked with a soft smile her eyes light up her face.

"You have snowflakes all over you." He wiped his hand across her shoulders.

"Duh, it's snowing." She pointed to the air with her chin.

"Duh, it makes you look even dorkier," Marcus said before shaking her face with is hand.

"Get out of here," she said with a giggle and a friendly shove.

~ * ~

"Jules, what are you doing?" Claire asked in a disapproving tone as she and Jimmy joined her the following Monday during lunch.

"What?" Julie shoved a forkful of salad into her mouth.

"You broke up with Todd," Claire seemed particularly bothered by the event.

"Yeah, I just wasn't into him."

"Isn't he the one you nicknamed 'Hercules'?" Jimmy added.

"I don't get it," her best friend said before asking. "What's your deal?"

Julie thought for a second that Claire's tone should insult her, but she let it go because even she had to admit. "I don't know."

"That guy was really into you."

"It just wasn't there," she said and then added, "I want what you two have."

Claire and Jimmy looked at each other, back to Julie, and then said simultaneously, "Since when?"

"Since always."

"No, sir," Claire exclaimed.

"What does that even mean?"

"It means that since I've known you, you have gone through boys like a…like I don't know what. You've had tons of boyfriends."

"Hyperbole much?" Julie questioned, still knowing her friend was right.

"You know what I mean. It's never bothered you before."

"I know."

Chapter Twelve

The cold, bleak days of Earth's winter were replaced by the warming sun, green grass, and blooming flowers in Seras. Julie took her seat near Redderick Bobo inside his tent. The women hovered around him in a lost trance.

It's like they can't function without him.

"Welcome back, my dear. I hope your time away was to your satisfaction."

"It was."

"Good, good."

She knew he was perturbed that she had been gone so long, but he once disappeared and never offered up where he went, so why should she.

He looked at her for a moment then as if he grew tired of waiting for her to say anything else, he began.

The next Elder to craft human life was Vestus, Elderess of the Sky.

She created two races. One was the Tarracks and the other was the Evadell. First, Vestus gathered three animals to a clearing in the woods: a bear, a cougar, and a hawk.

Under her command, the animals stood in peace with one another. Vestus waved her hand over them and they went into a deep sleep. "Thank you, my brothers, for your sacrifice." With her finger, she cut a sharp line across the hearts of the beasts.

Their blood spilled, mixing together. Vestus then traced two shapes of humans on the ground—one male, one female. The animals' blood filled the outlined forms. She whispered the ancient tongue of Heaven, finishing with, "I ask thee to rise."

The two creations rose to life. Vestus had the two eat their first meal of the sacrificed animals.

This was the beginning of the Tarrack tribe.

She left the Tarracks to turn her attention to a different race.

The Evandell were gathered from the moonlight. From the highest peak in Seras, Vestus collected beams in a clay jar filled with salt. Vestus rubbed her hands together, causing frictional heat and placed her hands in the container. She bowed humbly and released the beams and salt into the air with great force. Multitudes of Evandell people came to life to serve their elderess.

"So, this Vestus lady had both the Tarracks and Evandells? If your theory about Ostram is right, I bet this didn't make the other Elders happy," Julie said.

"I am impressed."

"I'm right?" Julie was surprised, which was quickly followed by a head bob.

"You are."

"Cool! Tell me what happened."

"I will. Allow me to finish, please."

Julie relented with pursed lips and squinted eyes.

Azahleah of the underworld named his new realm Speculus. In it, he created Death Walkers, eight in total. They were his spirit guides to the underworld. They would lead the dead to him until time to be joined with the others from Earth.

"How did he create them? You have all these stories, but you didn't say anything about how Death Walkers came to be," Julie said.

"That is because we do not know. He never revealed how he did it."

"He never told you?"

"No, it is said that he created more within the depths of the abyss, but none have witnessed these creations except possibly Bhjuda."

"Why him?"

"Bhjuda is the only person to journey into Speculus while alive."

"Oh, okay," Julie conceded. "Who's next?"

"I believe that is enough for the day."

"Are you kidding?" Julie stood in protest. "You're going to leave me hanging like that?"

"It is best that I leave you wanting more."

"That's crap!"

"Go find your Marcus."

She paused for a second. "He isn't my Marcus."

"Your Mr. Campbell."

"Why?"

"You are distracted. You are rushing things. You need to understand. In order to do that, you must have your mind in order."

Julie shook her head. "What are you talking about?"

"It is time for you to go." Redderick got up from his cushion and moved to the entrance of his tent. He pulled back the canvas door. "I will be here when you are ready."

"Fine!" Julie stormed off.

~ * ~

Julie and Marcus arrived back in his basement. Julie rushed ahead of him, got dressed and waited for him at the top of the stairs after he finished putting on his clothes. "I don't get it," Julie's rampage continued. "What does he mean I am rushing things?"

"I wasn't there. I don't know." He headed for the small apartment kitchen. "Do you want anything to drink?" he asked, opening the refrigerator.

"No, thanks. He always stops and says 'That is a story for another day.' I don't get it."

Marcus pulled out a pitcher of tea and poured it into a large glass. "Maybe he thinks he is going too fast for you or that he is confusing you."

"Do I look like I am easily confused?"

He smiled.

"Don't answer that." Julie pursed her lips and crinkled her nose.

"What did the two of you talk about?"

"Azahleah. He's the elder over the entire spirit world. Probably a lot like Hell."

"Are you sure about that?" Marcus slowed her down.

"What do you mean?"

Marcus stopped because he didn't want to tell her about his history with the Death Walker, Rinna. The same Death Walker who somehow found her way to Earth and tried to kill both of them last year, so he changed direction. "Remember what you learned in mythology class."

"You think Speculus is like Hades' Underworld? You think it has both the Elysium Fields and Tartarus?" Julie asked.

Her voice slowed, he knew he had her thinking and it was calming her down, which was a good thing, even if it were fleeting. "First, I'm impressed you actually pay attention in class, and yes, I think Speculus has both the good and the bad," he said.

"Hmm, I never thought about that," she cocked her head to the side. "I guess it does make sense, now that I think about it. Redderick said it's only a temporary resting place."

"Really? I never knew that."

"Yeah, and he made things called Death Walkers." Julie sat down and Shakespeare hopped on her lap.

"Things?" Marcus laughed.

"Well, I guess they're women, but not really." She pulled an apple from the bag and sank her teeth into the bright red juicy fruit.

"Why not 'really'?"

"Because they are spirits who help carry the dead to Speculus." Julie paused to pull her knees up on his couch and sat with her legs crisscrossed. "I guess they are really pretty too," she added.

Marcus listened with a smile.

"But then he told me he has never seen one. He said," at this she cleared her throat and put her hand on her chest, "'No, dear, I have only heard stories of their beauty from Lord Azahleah. You have to die before you can see a Death Walker'."

"You sound just like him."

"I know, right. But he always leaves me with something he doesn't tell me," Julie said, crunching her face.

"Like what?"

"I told ya about him only telling me that your dad was a great warrior and didn't tell me anymore," she reminded him.

"Yeah."

"Then, when he was telling me about the Death Walkers, he said no one living has ever seen them except," she stopped dramatically.

"Except…" Marcus played along.

"Except, he said there have been two people who have seen them without being dead."

"Two?" he asked tentatively.

"Yeah, but he never said who. He said it was a flippin' story for another time," she burst out waving her hands in an animated fashion.

"Well, I'm sure he has his reasons," Marcus tried to soothe his pupil, relieved that the old man had not told Julie he was one of the people who have seen a Death Walker while at the same time wondering who the second person was.

"Maybe, but it is frustrating," Julie said with a hint of sadness.

"What?" Marcus asked, picking up on her tone.

"Nothing," she hesitated.

"Tell me," he gently requested.

"She's in Speculus, huh?"

There was no need for her to state who 'she' was. Julie was talking about Callista. "Yes, she is there," Marcus said in a low voice.

"She'll be in the good part, right?"

"Of course she will. Callista was a great warrior," Marcus consoled her.

"But, being a great warrior isn't the reason why a person is good or bad," Julie said.

"No, but she was a good person too." He did his best to convince her Callista was wherever the good dead warriors went.

"But, what if…" she started.

"No. She was a good person and a great warrior. Anything she did before was erased. She ended up fighting for Heilshorn. Look at how much she did for you, and she died protecting you."

"Oh, God!" Julie burst into tears. "She died keeping me from getting killed!"

"No! I meant look at how much she taught you and worked with you," Marcus said, quickly moving to the couch and putting his arm around the sobbing girl, wishing he could take back what he just said.

"But it's my fault she died," she said between loud sniffles.

"Julie, she died doing what she wanted to do. She was a warrior, a fighter. She died a good death," Marcus repeated the philosophy of his old Skorei code.

"Stop! You're not helping!" Julie hopped up to her feet and turned her back on her mentor.

"I just mean…" he stopped. "I just…would you like to go see her?"

Julie faced him. Her eyes were bloodshot, her face streaked with tears. "What? No, I can't," she murmured.

"I will take you," he said in a somber voice.

"No, I just can't. I haven't even said her name out loud since that day."

"Maybe you should."

"No!" she said louder.

"Okay," Marcus resigned his request. "When you are ready, I'll be here."

"Thank you," Julie sighed, embracing him.

Chapter Thirteen

Still not happy with the idea of creating humans, Tolth decided to try his hand at creating animals. First, he began duplicating the animals of Earth and spread them across the new world. Twice, he created new types of animals. One was called leagros.

"I know that one. It's the one that looks like a hamster and rhino…" she looked awkwardly at Redderick Bobo. "…mated."

"Yes, so it does," the immortal chuckled.

Julie was pleased that she recognized the animals that were paired with elephants, rhinos, and ox to transport Griffus's catapults and other large structures during battles and construction.

"And then he created the lodear. They are a black, scaly animal with a large horn sticking out from the back of its neck."

"Marcus told me about those," she interrupted again. "He hunted them when he lived with the Greagons."

"Indeed," was Redderick's singular response.

After that, Tolth was satisfied by only recreating animals that were already in existence.

"Really? He was happy just duplicating lions and tigers and bears," she giggled before adding, "and a couple misfit animals?"

"For the time being. I do not want to get too far ahead of myself. I need to tell you about Lady Eryx."

The Elderess Eryx was worshiped by all men and women not recreated by her brothers and sisters. She gave man fire and became the goddess of fire, taking credit for giving man the gift of life and the flame to live. Because of that, she was loved more than most of the others. Tolth may have been just as popular since he was responsible for the land they had to grow their crops.

This did not sit well with Eryx. She became disillusioned with control over Seras. Her first order of business was to create the three Sisters of Tunlaw to be her eyes and ears of the world. They were vile creatures who devoured plants, animals, and humans in their wake.

"Marcus told me about them. Yuck!"

"So he did," Redderick smiled.

When word got back to Eryx that Tolth was being worshiped as much as she was, she became even more jealous. She formed an army of soldiers to go through villages and tear down statues of the other Elders and imprison or kill those who refused to worship her. When the forces of good stepped up to defend themselves against her army, Eryx created an even more powerful army. The Skorei.

"Oh, my gosh!" Julie exclaimed. "Those are the demons who pretty much wiped out every cool thing about Seras."

"They are. How did you hear about them, my dear?"

"Callista told me."

"I see."

"But she didn't tell me Eryx created them," she said trying to stroke his ego. "…or how they were created."

"That is a story—"

"For another day," Julie finished and started to get up from her seat on the pillowed couch.

"It is, but it is not the end of our day," he said and motioned for her to stay seated. "I will leave you with this final part of the story."

When Tolth saw what Eryx had done, he gave into his reluctance to create humans. He even made them from the same mold as Eryx's warriors. They are called the Corven.

"Hey, that's what Freya is!" Julie said.

"Yes, my child. Freya is a Corven. They are the female counterpart to…" he paused. "She is made from the very fabric of the warriors Eryx used to destroy man."

Julie nodded her head, thinking about what she had heard.

"They were a small band of healers for men to come to when hurt or dying. Azahleah protested at first, saying it went against his realm, but it was decided that they could not bring back anyone from the dead, just heal those without immediate fatal wounds. Azahleah was also upset that Tolth had made them in the form of women, thinking they would confuse the Corven with Death Walkers."

~ * ~

Julie sat quietly by the fireplace in Mr. Campbell's cabin. The flame flickered constantly, never growing weary from the long night, completely opposite from the young girl staring mesmerized by its warming glow.

"Can I ask you something?" Julie asked.

"Of course. You know you can ask me anything."

"So why did they choose me to be this savior thing for them? I'm just a girl."

"Wow!" he said, rubbing his hand through his hair. "Let's start with a tough one."

"I know. I'm sorry."

"Don't be." He moved from his spot against the wall so he could sit across from her. "I just don't have the answer. Remember, I went to Earth expecting to find a warrior-king, not a high school girl."

"Yeah, forget it. It doesn't matter."

"Yes, it does."

"No, it doesn't. I don't know what to think anymore. It feels like I'm falling apart." She pulled the furry blanket of soft rabbit pelt tighter around her body. "Sometimes I just want to curl up next to my mother and cry my eyes out. How's that for your savior?"

"I think it's perfectly normal."

"You do? Did you ever want to do that?"

"Well, no. I was raised differently, and my mother wasn't allowed to be near me."

"Huh?" She gave him a puzzled look. "I don't understand."

"Nothing. A story for another day."

"I hate when you do that." Julie turned to him in one swift movement, her fists held up in front of her.

"I know."

"Then why do you do it?"

"There's a time and a place for everything, and now, I'm more worried about you." Mr. Campbell's hands formed over her tightened grip.

How does he do that? Julie sighed and relaxed her fists.

"Let's get out of here," he suggested, making a movement to get up.

"No."

"No?" he asked, and let his weight shift back to the floor.

"No, I'm not ready yet. I want to hear more and learn more."

"You've changed your mind."

Julie swayed her head playfully. "I'm a girl; I'm allowed to do that."

"Do you want to train tomorrow or talk to Redderick?"

"Can't I do both?"

"I suppose." Mr. Campbell shrugged.

"Good."

"Then you should get some sleep. You just signed up for a busy day." He got up to leave.

"Where are you going?"

"I'm going to let you rest." He threw his long winter cloak over his shoulders.

"Oh, okay." Julie stood and adjusted her clothing as he opened the cabin door.

"Good night." Mr. Campbell looked over his shoulder and gave her a reassuring smile before walking away.

"Good night."

~ * ~

Queen Pallanex had swept in from her lower staircase, the one William knew was home for the majority of her pets and other secrets she kept from him. "Oh, what I would give to learn more about your mysteries," he purred under his breath before announcing his presence. "You called for me," William said in a cocksure voice. He sat in the middle of the queen's lush room. The blue lounge was his favorite place to recline as he waited for Queen Pallanex to make her entrance. He had spent the past few minutes watching the queen's spiders have free reign in a corner of her beautiful palace.

"I did. Your men are here," Queen Pallanex said. She was wearing a tight, golden gown. It had chainmail draped down from a neck collar attached to the front and back of the dress. Five peacock feathers adorned her crown of twisted gold strands.

William saw that she had a glow about her. She appeared radiant and nearly as young as the day he first did her bidding, which was just before the death of Canis, Marcus's father. "Good, where are they?" he asked, standing to greet her.

"Out doing my business. Now tell me that you have equally good news." She moved to the far end of the room where her throne sat gilded with intricate designs of animals and plants.

"Your business? What business do you have with my men?" he asked. Queen Pallanex's frown told him he needed to continue. "Where did you send them?"

"That is not important," Pallanex said with a certain level of disregard.

"What does that mean? Is my role so petty that you can wave me off as if I were an insect? I am very close. In fact, that army you

113

sent for your own business may have been what I needed for me to finish my work."

"How so?"

"What fun would it be if I told you that?"

"Tell me!" she commanded and then switched to more of a coo. "Tell me."

"If you insist. Upon their return, I will feed my army the soul of my pet, and you will have your army."

Pallanex was thrilled. She relaxed and her features turned soft. William knew that would change if she had any notion that he was planning on leaving at the first chance to march against Marcus and destroy everything and everyone he loves. *I will kill the Heart and then kill him.*

"You will have it ready by then?" Her smile was salacious. It snapped William out of his silent plot.

"I will," William answered. He returned her smile with a wink.

"You can complete it now?"

"Yes." He smiled salaciously.

"Good! What do you need from me?"

"I am so glad you asked," William said. He pulled her up from her throne and kissed her hard. The queen returned his passion. That brought a malicious grin from the Skorei commander.

He guided her to the throne.

She sat down with an uncharacteristic thud. "What do you want, William?"

William placed his hands on the gold crested armrest in the shape of a fowl. "I only require three things."

"Name them," she whispered.

"I want to know exactly what you are up to."

"In good time."

He pulled back. "When my new soldiers return and I produce the army you require?"

"Agreed," she nodded.

"I want a throne next to this one."

"When you hear of my plan, you will understand how trivial that demand is."

"Then I want a throne next to wherever your planned throne will be."

"It will be done."

"Good."

"And your third request?"

He looked at her with arrogance and a lust that he could not conceal behind the shining in his eyes. "More of this," he said, picking her up and carrying her to the royal blue lounge chair.

Chapter Fourteen

Julie and Marcus's swordplay rang through the tree line of the southern hills. Julie was using a double-handed grip attack while Marcus used one hand to defend against her with his black Evandell-made sword. "Okay, why is your sword different from mine…and everyone else's?"

"My father gave me this sword. It was part of my birthright."

She slowed down but kept up the training. "Does it have a name?"

"No, why would I name it?" Marcus struck Julie's sword with an overhead blow. She held up her weapon in defense.

"All famous weapons have names. You know, Thor had his hammer that I can't pronounce."

"Mjolnir."

"Yep, Bilbo had Sting; King Arthur had Excalibur."

"Wow! Who are you and what did you do with Julie?" he joked.

"I'm serious," she moaned.

"Well," Marcus said while fending off her advances both physical and mental. "First, mine is not famous, and second, that's only on Earth."

"But aren't you some famous warrior here?"

"Not exactly." Then he shifted the black handled blade back toward Julie. "Do you want me to name it?"

She guarded herself before going back to offense. "I think I do." She was pleased with her performance.

"What should I call it?" he asked with a slight laugh.

"I don't know. Something cool." She moved forward and made an overhead cut toward her teacher.

"Well, help me think of something cool." He rotated around her, defending against her attacks.

Julie swung hard, but her final effort was blocked and her sword dropped to the ground. Her hand stung, and a gash appeared on her arm from the impact of the blow.

"Ugh! How do you do that?" she asked in defeat. Her hands were on her knees and she panted in exhaustion. "How 'bout the Julie-killer?"

"That's not even funny. Come on let's go again." He sheathed his sword and shook his arms in preparation.

"Are you kidding? I'm sore from head to toe." Julie scrunched her face and pursed her lips.

"That is the only way you're going to get better."

"Not if I can't move my arms." She held up her hand to show him the crimson cut across the meaty part of her palm.

"Julie, I'm so sorry!" He took her by the arm and held it at eye level. "I didn't mean to—"

"It's okay. That's what happens, I guess."

"Okay, what if I give you a week off?"

"Here or there?" She looked up at him. His blues eyes showed serious concern.

"Here." He let go of her hand. She bent over to catch her breath.

"No workouts, no sword fighting, no training?" she asked in reservation.

"None. And I'll let you name my sword if you want."

"What is this? What's the catch?"

"No catch."

"You told me that there's always a catch."

"I did, didn't I?" He laughed. Her joking must have signaled that she wasn't in serious pain. "Well, this time there's not. I think you need a break."

"Cool! When do we go back?" She stood erect in excitement.

"After you beat me down the hill and back."

"You lied! You said there wasn't a catch."

"I didn't lie. All you have to do beat me."

"I hate you." She wrinkled her nose into a growl.

"No, you don't."

Then she surrendered. "No, I don't."

~ * ~

"Okay, so what's the deal?" Julie asked Redderick Bobo a few hours later after her training with Marcus. "Oh, gross!" She had taken the immortal by surprise when she threw open his tent flap and stormed inside. The harem scattered, leaving him shirtless, laying on his back on the pillowed bed.

"The deal? I am not sure I know what you mean," he answered.

She regrouped her thoughts from the grotesque display in front of her, drew a deep breath, and said, "I just cut myself working out with Marcus and…I don't know, a minute or two later it was perfectly healed. Look!" She held up her arm and rotated the back of her forearm to Redderick. "And that's not the first time it has happened. It did it once when Callista…" She stopped. It still pained her to say Callista's name. "When Callista accidently hit me in the arm and I thought I broke it. It took a little longer, but it healed. Then when I cut my hand when the giant hit me, I was fine by the time I got back to my house." The thought of that night, everything thing that happened, fighting with Marcus flooded her mind, but she refrained from letting it distract her. "But it's happening faster now. What gives?"

118

"My dear, you are getting stronger. You have special gifts, the gift of healing, among others." He rose from his position on the bed and reached for his vest.

"I don't get it."

"The stronger you get the more you will notice that wounds and such will not last much longer than it takes to say your name."

"So, I can't be hurt?"

"Oh, no, you can be hurt. The deeper the wound, the longer it takes to heal, but as long as you are breathing, your body will restore itself."

"Is that why I was never sick or in the hospital growing up?" He walked over to a counter and poured himself a drink.

"Precisely, my dear."

"How 'bout this big freaking zit on my forehead?" Julie semi-joked with a laugh. The immortal ignored her. *Maybe he doesn't know what a pimple is.* She shrugged.

"Marcus, er, your Mr. Campbell has the same gift," he said. "Would you like a drink?"

"No, thank you," she answered before directing her attention to his previous statement. "He does? Are we the same?"

"No, my child. The two of you are nothing alike, but that ability is one of the threads that bonds—"

"Bonds? I don't get it?"

He sat down and offered her a seat. "Bond is the wrong word," Redderick said. Julie could swear he stumbled in his answer. "Link, is a better word. The two of you have a link to one another. That is why it was so easy for him to find you, and why you found it easy to trust him."

Julie thought about that first day in the basement. The pentagram on the floor. How she thought it was a demonic sign, not the portal it turned out to be. "Easy to trust, isn't how I would describe it."

"But you do."

"I do now, but when I saw the symbol on the floor, I was scared to death and wanted to run as fast as I could." She sat down near him but kept her distance.

"But you did not."

"No."

"You trust him," he said with a certain gleam in his eye. "And you trusted him enough to ignore your fear and step into the Elder's symbol with him, not knowing what would happen."

"Okay, yes, that is all true, but that doesn't help me understand what you mean by having a bond."

"No, perhaps not, but the bond I referred to was important to Marcus figuring out it was you, and for you trusting him enough to go with him."

"Why?"

"Ah, my dear, none of us can bend the mysterious rules of the universe."

Julie still felt Redderick was holding back something from her, but she relented in pursuing it further. "Fine. I have no idea what that means. So what little story do you have for me today?"

"My so-called 'little story' is the first fight between Lord Tolth and Lady Eryx. They stood on the temple dais...

"What are you doing?" Tolth asked. Eryx was looking down from the dais to the world under them. Her worshipers were constructing a statue of the beautiful Eldress.

"I am watching over my people," she answered with a hint of disdain.

"Eryx, I am worried about you. You have not been yourself since we decided to create life."

"Who are you to tell me such things?" Her anger was evident. "I am doing what we should all be doing. These people are to do our bidding. We created them to worship us."

"You remind me of the fallen one."

"Do not start with me. He was a great angel and we were lucky to serve under him…"

"No! He wanted nothing but to be higher than our Father!" Tolth slammed his fist into a marble altar. "He got what he deserved."

"He wanted nothing but to not worship humans and their filth!" Eryx responded just as harshly.

"So says you," Tolth spewed towards the obstinate elderess and turned away in disgust.

"So says you," Eryx said, glaring intensely. Her eyes looked like black holes that could suck in anything and nothing would come out alive.

"Wait, who are they talking about?" Julie interrupted.

"The angel, Lucifer," Redderick answered.

"The devil?" Julie exclaimed loudly.

"Yes, he has been called that."

"He was cast down from Heaven for disobeying God."

"And Eryx had helped defeat him and his followers. That is why she and the other Elders were rewarded Seras."

"Yeah, I remember that part of the story, but why are they fighting about Lucifer now?"

"Because Eryx was a sympathizer."

"A sympathizer?"

"She thought Lucifer was correct in not wanting to serve humans. She did not like the way he planned on doing it, and that is why she did not join him."

"That sucks," Julie exclaimed.

"I am not sure what that means, but I am sure I agree," Redderick chuckled.

Julie decided it would be useless to try to explain to the other-worldly man the meaning of her expression. "Now I really hate Eryx."

"Please, pay attention. It is important for you to know this."

"Okay."

The springtime of their existence was dwindling away. They were called back to Heaven and reprimanded by their Father for the things they had done.

The five appeared in columns of white smoke in His presence. They bowed gracefully to the Holy One. As they stood in the congregation of the Almighty, He placed judgment on what had become of Seras and rendered this verdict and warning to them.

"How long will you judge unjustly and show favoritism to the wicked? Defend the poor and fatherless! Do justice to those who are oppressed and suffering! Deliver the poor and needy! Free them from the hand of the wicked! They neither know nor understand. They stumble about in darkness; all the foundations of the world crumble." Then, *He finished with this:* "You are like gods. All of you are children of the Most High, but now, I tell you this, you shall die like mortals and fall like men."

After the decree, Tolth met with Ostram on the stone dais that overlooked Seras below. "We need to do something about Eryx."

"I thought it was made very clear to all of us that we need to rethink what we have done. "*The yellow-haired elder plopped into a stone chair.* "Eryx knows she is being watched."

"No, that only slowed her down. We need to stop her." *Tolth moved closer to his friend.* "She is waging war on Seras and creating idols."

"The elegance of pure power is lost on the weak of spirit."

Tolth stared at him and shook his head. "This is no time for your cleverness. Look at what she has done. She created an army of men, and when we stopped that, she created an army of demons."

"And you created the Corven to cut the number of her army in half and heal those who were injured."

"The people of Seras are dying. How much worse is it going to get?"

"Why do you want to, as you said, 'wage war' on our sister?" Ostram asked, remaining seated as he watched Tolth pace back and forth.

"Did you not hear our Father? It is already too late for us. We will die like mortal men because of our actions. We have lost Seras. Eryx has done this to us all for nothing."

Ostram stood. "You believe she will not stop?"

Tolth turned to his brother. "I know she will not stop. Whatever she has planned will be the end of Seras."

"Then we must act fast. Eryx is too smart to wait for us to make a move."

"Thank you, my brother. Go to Azahleah and I will go to Vestus. The four of us will have to put an end to her evil doings."

As the changing of the seasons, in the wake of the merriment of spring, came the burning anger of harsh summer.

"I want no part of this," Azahleah said. His human likeness took on the form of a skinny man with brown hair and lizard-green eyes. He wore a ragged cloak of black and brown that covered his entire torso. "Eryx is my sister. She does me no harm."

"You mean she gives you plenty to do," Ostram chided.

"Very well, yes, she and I have a partnership that is prosperous," he cackled.

"Look at you!" Tolth roared. "This is why we will die like dogs. You are taking pleasure in killing humans."

Azahleah stood firm. "Ha, that is where we differ. You see, my realm is all about the dead. If no one dies, no one is there to worship me."

Vestus spoke from behind Tolth. "What do you want from us, Tolth?" The tall, dark-skinned woman had a slow, soft voice. Her almond shaped eyes stared at him in deep earnest. "Her demons have captured or killed many of my Evandell. She has broken my trust."

"She has done more than that. I know that Eryx is planning something on a large scale that will destroy Seras and Earth." He checked to make sure he had their attention. "Her plans may even expand beyond that."

"You still have not told us what you would like for us to do," Vestus said.

"I want to exile Eryx from our ranks," Tolth answered.

Azahleah jerked his head in surprise. Ostram closed his eyes and held his mouth. The elder's lips turned white.

"Why would I want to help you do that?" Azahleah scoffed. He hopped around the dais in a fit of rage.

"You are asking a lot, brother," Vestus said in a composed manner. She crossed her arms in front of her chest.

"What Tolth is trying to say is we need to have a plan to stop her and whatever her plan is," Ostram said, trying to regain the other two's confidence. "...if it comes to that."

"If it comes to that, by then it will be too late," Tolth argued.

"No," Ostram stopped his rant. "If we are prepared, we will have the power to overcome her plan." He then directed his attention back to Vestus and Azahleah. He took Vestus by the hand and kissed it.

"Are you trying to charm me?" she cooed.

"Indeed, I am." He smiled. "Is it working?"

"It might."

"Your charm will not work on me," Azahleah said. He sat on the edge of an arm of a thick chair and crossed his leg.

Tolth walked over to him. He caught on to what Ostram was doing. "No, of course not. But, my brother, please listen. With your help, if the time comes that Eryx oversteps her bounds..." He stopped to think about the fact that she had already crossed those borders many times over but held his tongue to that point. "...we will be ready to strike against her."

Azahleah hopped from his seat. "Very well, what would you like me to do?"

Tolth looked at Azahleah, then to Vestus and Ostram before returning his gaze back to Azahleah. "I would like to suggest that we create individual gifts that can be used to assist in defending Seras and stopping whatever evil she plans on using against us and Seras."

"I see." He rolled his hands together excitedly. "What kind of gifts?"

Ostram spoke up. "I know you still have access to the old world."

"Indeed, I do." Azahleah looked at him in curiosity.

"Then use that power. It is a gift that you alone have and would be useful in times of need." Ostram was masterful at handling the off-centered elder.

"What would you suggest for me?" Vestus said. She was not convinced that Tolth's idea was in the best interest for Seras, but she did not fully trust Eryx either.

"You are wise and resourceful, my dear Vestus. I am sure whatever you come up with will be satisfactory," Ostram answered with a bow.

"Can we agree to meet back here with our gifts?" Tolth asked. "How long will you need?"

"The question is how long will you need?" Azahleah threw it back to Tolth with a cynical grin.

The Elderess Vestus interjected. "I will not need much time."

"Then neither do I," Azahleah shot back.

Tolth began to speak, but Ostram held up his hand to quiet him. "It is not a competition. We will reconvene in the period of a season. Come back then with your gift."

"As you desire." Azahleah bowed low and vanished in a flume of smoke.

Vestus paused for a moment. "I will do this, but I fear you are making a mistake."

"Sister, I hope that it does not come to war with Eryx," Tolth said.

"Preparing for war is one step toward causing it." She hugged her brothers and left in her usual fashion.

Ostram and Tolth remained. Ostram spoke first. "I have work to do, as do you. I will see you soon."

"Thank you, my brother," Tolth said as Ostram vanished in a cloud of white.

Tolth spoke. "Did you record all of that?" The clandestine immortal, Redderick Bobo, appeared.

"Every word, my lord."

Chapter Fifteen

"Five are the Elders with their gifts born in the black of night," Redderick Bobo recited from the ancient Seras prophecy. "Five are the Elder's gifts hidden to set Seras right. Five Elders pitted beneath an angry sun. Blood will flow. Flesh and blade become one. The Blood is given to ease time; The Breath known to free men's minds; The Bones to merge distance and space; The Body a destined warrior, the Solia Custor, out of place, forged in battle with one true oath: protect Tolth's final gift, the Heart of Seras, our final hope."

Julie sat silently still on the pillowed couch. She had her hand over her mouth in her own personal style of having her pinky under her nose.

"Have you heard this before?" he asked her, unable to interpret her lack of reaction.

"No," was her laconic answer.

The look on Redderick's face told her what he was going to say even before he said, "I have to say I am surprised."

"So what does it all mean?" Julie asked. She readjusted, placing her elbows on her knees and resting her cheeks in her palms.

"It is something I wrote following the disclosing of the Elder's gifts. It should have been shared with you by now."

"Well, it hasn't. So now you can tell me."

"Very well." He stood and lit a candle on a nearby mantel. "Vestus was the first to reveal her gift—The Blood of Vestus, an oil compound that when warmed by fire spreads its glow and slows time."

Julie sat up straight. She couldn't help but interject. "I know it's the candle Mr. Campbell lights just before we leave for Seras."

"Yes, it has been changed to candle form for easier travel. It allows the two of you to travel to Seras without suspicion of being gone, but it can do much, much more," Redderick added.

"Such as?"

"Imagine what a warrior could do against an army by simply slowing time."

"But the warrior would be under its influence too." Julie cocked her head and twisted her mouth to one side.

"Ah, but there are some that are immune to its effects." He winked and continued. "The Blood of Vestus to ease time. Next, Ostram gave The Breath of Ostram. It--"

"I know what it does." Julie frowned. "I've seen it in action. Heck, he even used it on me so I can understand your language. So we can move on. I don't like what it does."

"But my dear, it is a wonderful gift. What Marcus did was very necessary to bring you here, and he could have done more than he did."

"Like what?"

"Did he use it on you to make you come to Seras?" Redderick asked.

"No."

"Did he use it to make you stay forever?"

"No," she answered a little louder, adjusting uncomfortably in her seat.

"Did he use it to make you forget where you are from or who your parents are?"

"No, oh gosh, no! It can do all of that?" Julie gave him a look of panic. "I've seen what it did to Mr. Christian, and I know he accidentally killed a guy, but that was just because he didn't know."

"As I said, he could have done much more. It shows great restraint to wield so much power and not use it to its fullest potential," he said. "Your Mr. Campbell cares for you a great deal, and what he did, he did with the purpose to find you, meet you, and bring you to Seras safely and by your free will. You should be very grateful. Others may not have been so strong."

Julie let those words sink in. *He's right. Mr. Campbell had all of this power and he only used it when he had to.*

The immortal spoke again, "The Breath is known to free men's minds. Azahleah pulled his gift out of a bag. They were the Six Stones of Speculus."

"I know about them too. There are three here and three at Mr. Campbell's. That's how we travel back and forth. It's how he found me," she said before finishing in a whisper, "And how he almost got hit by my dad's car."

"Indeed, but like all of the other gifts, there is more. Marcus appeared to you because he was looking for you. He could have traveled anywhere he wanted. It will take you to your heart's desire. He wanted to find you, and that is where the portal took you."

"Really? I didn't know that." Then she changed the topic. "Why does it remove all of your clothes?"

"Because, my dear, there are only certain things and certain people that can pass through the portal; the Heart, you; Marcus, the Solia Custor; the other gifts from the Elders; and anything blessed by one or more of the Elders." He quickly added, "The Bones to merge distance and space. The other immortal, Bhjuda Heilshorn, had to retrieve the six stones."

"Wait, why? You just said he presented his gift to the rest of them."

"He did, but when Tolth did not present his gift right away, Azahleah refused to share his with them."

"What was Tolth's gift?" Julie asked without stopping to think about it.

"You, my dear girl." Redderick laughed.

"Oh, yeah." Julie was embarrassed. She shook her head, disgusted with herself. "And Mr. Campbell was Eryx's gift," she added to save face.

"Yes, that happened before Tolth told the others about the plan for his gift. He convinced the other four Elders to make one of Eryx's warriors into her gift. There would be a sign. The warrior would appear to one of the Elders in the heat of battle and that would be the start of the prophecy."

"I don't get it."

"The Body a destined warrior, the Solia Custor, out of place, forged in battle with one true oath, to protect Tolth's final gift--the Heart of Seras, our final hope. The Body of Eryx was going to be a brave warrior, one forged in battle. The Elders convened to place an enchantment on Ostram, who volunteered under Tolth's encouragement to be the one to appear in front of the warrior and mark him as the Solia Custor."

"Oh…"

Redderick began to fill in the gaps.

"My brother," Tolth said to Ostram as the four stood in a circle. They gathered around the three previously received gifts: Ostram's container of liquid to influence the minds of men, Vestus's oil to slow time, and Azahleah's stones to transport from one realm to another. "I believe it should be you to show yourself to the guardian."

"You know what you are asking?" Ostram questioned.

"Why him?" Azahleah asked, breaking from the group.

"Would you come up from the abyss to do such a thing?" Tolth asked him.

Azahleah shrunk away. "No, but it would be nice to be asked."

Vestus held up her hand to stop the argument. "Ostram is a fine choice. I would not want the honor. We have no idea how long this will take. He must live on Seras until that time comes, giving up his place here."

"Very well," Azahleah said. "Now that you say it like that...Ostram is the best choice." He smiled and moved back into the circle.

The three gathered around Ostram. They chanted in the language of the angels and placed their hands on Ostram. He was filled with light. Each gave him a small dose of their celestial legacy. He dropped to his knees.

"I hope this is worth it," Ostram said. Bitterness filled his voice. He knew it was for the best, he just hated that it had to happen.

"Thank you, my brother." Tolth embraced him. "Your sacrifice will mark the Solia Custor, our lone guardian."

"Now it is your turn," Azahleah said to Tolth.

"Not yet," he responded.

"What do you mean?" Vestus asked.

"My gift is going to be spread out in the Alpha world to be claimed later."

"What does that mean?" Vestus asked.

"Why is your gift so special?" Azahleah was indignant.

"My gift will be hidden from Eryx, and it will be retrieved by the Solia Custor when the time comes."

"No! That was not the deal. We were to present our gifts now. I want to see your gift." Azahleah leapt around in anger.

"That was not the deal. I cannot show you my gift yet. My gift, My Heart, will be born when evil is nearing its peak. The Solia Custor will go to Earth and bring it back to Seras. It will be his job to protect it, train it and prepare it for the evil Eryx will unleash here. And with any luck, it will defeat Eryx, saving Seras, Earth and Heaven from the evil she will bring forth."

"Unacceptable!" Azahleah screeched. He scooped up his bag of stones and vanished before their eyes.

Vestus looked at Ostram in his weakened stat, and to Tolth. "What have you done here, Tolth?"

"I am trying to save us."

"You have destroyed us."

"Sister," Tolth pleaded.

"No!" her voice echoed through the chamber. *"We trusted your guidance and wisdom. We followed you to this end, and look at what you have done."*

"No!" he barked back. *"I am fixing what Eryx has done. You heard our Father. What she has done to Seras, she has destroyed in the name of being worshiped. The cries of the suffering and poor are her doing. The suffering she caused--"*

"Stop, Tolth!" Vestus yelled. *"You are placing this on her, but remember our Father blamed all of us for what Seras has become."* With that, the dark skinned elderess left.

"That is what I am trying to fix," Tolth said to himself.

"I know, my brother," Ostram patted him on the shoulder. *"They will come around."*

"And if not?"

"Well, you still have me." Ostram smiled though his powers were gone. *"Now, can you give me a ride to Seras. It seems I will be stuck there for quite a while."*

"I am sorry, my brother. It was the only way."

"I know, and I will help you in your quest to right our wrongs."

"Thank you." Tolth turned to the back of the dais. *"Redderick!"*

"Yes, your lordship."

"Tell your brother I have a mission for him."

Yes, sir."

"Tell him that he must go to Azahleah's abyss and retrieve the Stones of Speculus." Tolth reached out for Ostram's hand and in a funnel cloud, they were gone.

Chapter Sixteen

"Hi, Marcus, I'm glad you could make," Julie's dad said as he opened the front door of his house. He stuck out his hand and Marcus shook it.

Julie came bounding down the steps with her shoulder length brown hair pulled back in a ponytail and dressed in a green, white, red, and gold tie-dyed shirt and dark blue shorts. "Well, I do declare, look what the cat dragged in," Julie said in a mock southern debutante accent.

"Uh, hi, Julie."

"I just can't believe we only have one more quarter of school. It's just flying by," Julie continued her southern belle voice as Marcus stepped into the entryway.

He knew she was trying hard to pretend that they had not just been in his basement less than an hour ago following another grueling day of practicing her sword fighting skills. He wasn't sure why she decided to talk the way she was.

"Where is this coming from?" Phillip asked, giving his daughter a strange look.

Julie shrugged. "I don't have the faintest idea." She stopped just short of the banister and began fanning herself with her hand. "If I had known we were going to have gentlemen guests, I would have put on my corset." She smiled.

"Where did you come from?" Phillip shook his head.

"I do declare, father, you should know because you raised me." Julie laughed.

Phillip moved toward the kitchen still shaking his head. "Okay, Scarlett."

"So, how was school today?" Marcus asked as he entered the family home and followed Phillip toward the kitchen. He wanted to help her continue her deceit without breaking into a *Gone with the Wind* accent.

"Well, Mr. Campbell," Julie said in the slow, sugary drawl, "I'll wait to see how my test goes next week. I know a certain mythology teacher who likes to give really hard tests." Julie scrunched her face and hopped into the nearest chair at the table.

"I have a feeling you're talking about me." Marcus winked and took a seat beside her.

"Good." She lost the southern accent. "Promise me you won't have some impossible exam like the lame one you had last year for Freshman Comp."

"No promises."

"Mr. C!" Julie squealed. "You have to. I have so many other classes I have to study for. At least give me a heads up to what's going to be on it."

"Julie, he can't do that," her mother reprimanded her. "Hello, Marcus." He stood politely. "I'm so glad you could join us," Michelle said, giving him a side hug.

"Thank you for inviting me." Marcus sat back down.

"I could use some help, young lady." Michelle gave a side-glance to Julie.

"Mercy sakes, mother," Julie said, slipping back into her southern belle drawl. "You're trying to wear me to the bone."

"Where did that come from?" Michelle asked, looking at both Julie and Phillip. Julie got up to help set the table.

"She gets it from your side of the family."

"Not hardly."

As the family sat down with the teacher, Julie's mother changed topics. "Have you heard about the pageant they are having for the town celebration in July?"

"I have heard a little about it," Marcus answered between bites of pork chop and green bean casserole.

"Phil is on the committee to set it up."

"We decided to call it the Chocolate Festival," Phillip added. "We figured Circleville had their Pumpkin Show, Marion had the Popcorn Festival, Reynoldsburg Tomato Festival, Hartford Village Days, Sunbury has Sizzle and Sound, and Delaware has their Little Brown Jug--we needed our own identity."

"I see. I like the idea."

"Ask him what else they are going to have," Julie prodded before taking a big, uncomfortable drink.

"We're going to have a pageant and name a queen and her court," Phillip said. "Not nearly as bad as my daughter makes it sound."

"In fact," Michelle chimed in. "I think Julie should be one of the contestants."

"Mom!" Julie protested. Her lips tightened and her brown eyes grew large in shock.

"See what I mean. I wish you would convince my daughter to try out for it. It would be good for her."

"I'll try, but you know she is very stubborn," Marcus said.

Julie gave him a stern look.

"I'm glad someone else noticed," Michelle said.

"I don't know what you two are talking about," Julie said, twisting strands of hair around her finger. "But I don't want to be the only person signing up for a pagcant. I bet no one else does it."

"How can you be sure?" her father asked.

"Because it's awkward."

"Why would it be awkward?" Michelle asked. She moved her plate forward and folded her arms in front of her with her elbows on the table.

"Just because something has never been done before doesn't mean you shouldn't do it," Marcus said tentatively, hoping his position didn't feel like they were ganging up on her.

"What if I told you that more than a dozen girls have already signed up?" Phillip asked before Julie could respond, though Marcus could see the disappointment in her eyes.

"I would say that I would think about it." Julie grimaced.

"Oh, that makes me so happy!" Michelle said.

"I said, I would *think* about it."

"I know you will make the right decision."

"Mom," Julie said, rolling her eyes.

"I'll stop talking about it, now."

"Thank you." As Julie said that, her steak knife jumped as she was cutting her pork chop. The blade raked across her index finger, leaving it wide open between her knuckle and the first joint. "Oh, crap!"

"Oh, my God!" Julie's mother screamed. She jumped up to take care of her daughter.

"Are you okay?" Marcus asked in a panic.

Phillip got up to get a rag. In a few seconds, he was pressing a wet, cold towel on the bleeding wound.

"Phil, should we take her to the emergency room?" Michelle asked. "It looked pretty deep."

"No, I'll be okay. I'm so clumsy." She extended her hand and closed it again.

"I really think we need to get you to a hospital."

"Mom!"

"What can I do to help?" Marcus asked.

"Nothing, I'm okay. Look, it's already stopped bleeding." After saying that, Marcus and Julie became painfully aware of her parents' expression.

What was she going to say to her parents? Marcus thought. "It must have been a surface cut. You know how those pesky things bleed." He tried deflecting the awkwardness.

"Yeah, it wasn't that bad," Julie played along with the lie. "I'm such a baby."

"It was deeper than a surface cut," Michelle argued.

"But look." Julie rubbed her free hand over the area. "There's barely a mark."

"It bled an awful lot." Phillip held up the dishrag he used to stop the bleeding. The white towel was now crimson.

"The blood vessels on the hands and face are so sensitive. They bleed like crazy. You know," Marcus continued to ramble. "That's why big time wrestlers always have blood running down their faces. It's easy to manipulate the vessels."

The three looked at him. Julie gave him a look that said, *What in the world are you talking about?*

Later that evening, Julie uttered those words as they stood on the porch together. "What in the world were you talking about in there?"

"I have no idea," Marcus said with a slight laugh.

"Have you even ever watched big-time wrestling?"

"No. It must have been something I picked up from Mr. Christian or Lukas."

Julie frowned. The mention of those two names still bared a certain sadness at what had happened to them. "Well, whatever it was, it worked. I guess we have one of them to thank."

"I thank them every day," Marcus said as he walked down the porch steps.

"You do?" Julie leaned over the railing.

"Yes, of course. I thank them every day for their sacrifice. Without them, I would have never found you. I wish I knew then what I know now and it wouldn't have cost them their lives, but to ignore what they gave would be selfish of me."

"I will stop by tomorrow," Julie suggested.

"No, take the day off. You need it."

"Are you sure?"

"Yep. You earned it."

"Cool."

He left her after a round of goodbyes, made his way back home, poured himself a glass of milk, sat on the couch with Shakespeare in his lap, and fell asleep.

~ * ~

"That is impeccable," said a junior boy who was sitting with Jimmy and Claire in biology class the following Monday as Julie approached the table they were going to be sharing.

"What's impeccable?" she asked as she sat down.

"You, Mike thinks you're peccable," Jimmy said with a hardy laugh.

The boy with curly blond hair and green eyes got very embarrassed. "Seriously?"

"Yeah, right," Julie said rolling her eyes.

Claire moved her eyes from Julie to the boy to signal that Julie should say something to Mike.

"Um, hi," she said awkwardly.

"Hi," the boy responded.

"What's wrong with you?" Claire whispered.

Jimmy must have known that was his cue to find something else to do. He and Mike left the table to get the needed supplies for the day's lesson.

Julie blew out a deep breath. "Nothing, I'm having a bad day."

"I guess. You look like you got hit by a truck. Plus, you totally missed Mike flirting with you."

"What? When?"

"Just now. When was the last time you had a boyfriend?"

"I don't keep track of things like that."

"Well, I do. Too long."

"What?"

"I'm serious. Ever since, I don't know, fifth grade, you have had nonstop boyfriends. Now, it's been, what, one this whole year? What happened? What's been happening?"

"Nothing. I've been busy."

"That's what I keep hearing."

"What?"

"Nothing."

"Tell me?"

"Okay, fine. You don't call me, you don't text, you don't get online, you don't come over…I can't remember the last time we had a sleepover."

The science teacher interrupted Claire's rant with a lecture about things they would need to know for their next test: "…and I'm sure you will need to know that the lips are called bilabial and they are articulators and be able to tell me what that means."

Jimmy leaned over to Claire and said, "Dude, you have beautiful articulators."

Claire smirked. Julie smiled. She knew her best friend was in between wanting to smack him and kiss him.

"I want that," Julie whispered. "Huh?" Claire asked.

"Huh, um, nothing…" Julie sank in her chair. *Maybe I said that a little too loud.*

~ * ~

Later that day Julie and Mr. Campbell exited the portal in Seras. They were about to go their separate ways when Julie stopped in her tracks. "You know, I was thinking."

"Oh, this should be good," he said with a smile.

"You need a T.V."

"Why?" Marcus raised his eyebrow.

"That way you can actually watch big-time wrestling and know what you're talking about."

"What makes you think I would watch--"

"You also need a phone," Julie continued, not allowing him to finish. He opened his mouth to speak, but Julie kept going. "That way I can call you or text you when I'm coming over or not going to be able to make it. Don't you get tired of me popping in unannounced?"

"Well, I--"

"I think it would make our lives easier. It's only fair to you."

"Okay…"

"Okay, cool. I'll help you when we go back." Julie skipped away, leaving Marcus to do whatever he did when she was with Redderick Bobo.

Chapter Seventeen

"What have you done, sister?" Eryx screamed at Vestus. The two elderesses were standing in a fertile clearing in the middle of a forest near a riverbed.

"What have I done? Look at what you have caused!" Vestus fired back. "You were the one who created those monsters. They murdered my precious Evandells."

"They did not kill all of them," Eryx said wistfully.

"No," the sarcasm oozed from Vestus's lips. "They enslaved the rest of them to make weapons."

"Be thankful my demons have not touched the Tarracks yet."

"Yet?" Vestus screamed. "Enough is enough. Do you see what you are doing? Why are you causing this destruction?"

"I know what you have done!" Eryx raged. "You, Tolth, Ostram and Azahleah, I know about your pact."

"Then you do not know everything." Vestus smiled. "Azahleah refused to cooperate."

"Good for him. At least there is one with sense."

"The funny thing is, Eryx, is that I would support you had you not destroyed my people." Vestus turned away from her.

"If your people would have worshiped me, I would have left them alone."

"Worship you?" Vestus whipped back around. "What gives you the right to have the people I created worship you?"

"I am the Elderess of Fire. Without me, there would be no food, no weapons, no warmth in the cold. They should all worship me."

"Do you know how crazy that sounds? Do you know how much that sounds like--"

"Yes, I do!" Eryx lifted her hands above her head. "You said you would support me, sister. I aim to take out Tolth and Ostram. Do you support me now?"

Vestus paused. It was a mistake to wait that long. Eryx attacked her before another word was spoken. A lightning blast tore through Vestus's body. She careened into a tree. The tree splintered and fell.

The elderess got to her feet. "It does not have to be this way." She raised her hands to shoulder level to attack. She clapped her hands together. A gush of wind swept Eryx off of her feet. Vestus uprooted a tree and swung it down on her sister. The tree fragmented across her body.

Eryx shook off the effects. "I'm afraid it does." She wound up again and struck Vestus with another bolt, sending her reeling into the ground, causing a large divot of rock and dirt. It gave Eryx an idea. "If you are not with me, you are against me."

Vestus sent a flash of light, knocking Eryx back and temporarily blinding her. Vestus followed up with a flurry of punches. Eryx fell hard.

"This is foolish," Vestus said. "Stop what you are doing and we can return to the way things were."

"The way things were?" Eryx laughed. She struck Vestus with a mighty backhand. Vestus twisted and toppled, making another small crater. "The way things were was not working for me."

"Because you want power?" Vestus climbed to her feet.

"Yes," Eryx answered and hammered Vestus with a thundering bolt of fire. "And love." She followed with a strike of her hand.

Vestus stood again in defiance. "Love? Do you think killing every person except demons will offer you love?" Before she had a chance to return the volley, Eryx plowed into her with her full force, driving her back into the hole.

The Elderess of the Air tumbled back in defeat. "Do you plan to kill me, sister?"

Eryx stood over her and began chanting in the ancient tongue. She paused long enough to say, "No, dear Vestus, I will not kill you. I will only make you wish you were dead." With that, Eryx continued her intonation.

Vestus felt her limbs grow tired and heavy. "No, Eryx, you would not."

Eryx chanted louder with a quicker tempo.

The ground rose and began engulfing Vestus. Fire formed, wielding the two masses. Her body entwined with the rock. It rippled as she breathed. It planted firm where she stood. "No, sister, you cannot do this to me." The land closed in all around her. "No!" her voice echoed through the rock until finally no sound was heard.

"I can, my sister, and I did." Eryx stood at the entrance of the cavern. She could hear weeping from deep within. "I left you alive because while you betrayed me, I feel you only did so because you were led astray. I will not show mercy a second time."

Eryx left in a clouded flume.

"Oh, my gosh!" Julie exclaimed. "What happened to her?"

"Has Marcus told you about his trip to the talking cave?" Redderick moved a little closer to his pupil.

"Oh, yeah. That was Vestus, was it?" Julie shifted away from him. "She was mad. She almost killed him instead of giving him the Breath of Vestus."

"Indeed, she did."

Then Julie remembered something else from the story. "Wait. Didn't she have a Greagon with her?"

"She did. When Ostram heard what had happened to Vestus, he sent one of his creations to be her eyes, ears, and hands. It was his way of making up for what had happened up to her."

"Oh, okay. That makes sense."

"Good, but we are getting ahead of ourselves. That happened after the battle between Ostram, Tolth and Eryx."

"Azahleah didn't take part?"

"No. As I told you, Azahleah buried himself in Speculus and has never been seen since. We are not even sure if Bhjuda saw him when he ventured into the abyss to recover the stones."

"I get that he wasn't happy, but why didn't he join, especially after what Eryx did to Vestus?"

"By then it was too late, and Azahleah only worried about his self-preservation."

"You mean he was a coward," Julie said. She crossed her arms in front of her chest in disgust.

Redderick didn't say anything derogatory about Azahleah and continued his story.

Their world was torn, twisted and destroyed through their actions. The changes happened like the leaves on a tree deep in the light of fall.

Lord Tolth met Eryx inside one of her temples. She stood in front of a large jade sculpture of herself. Flowers and fruit laid in front of the statute and flames burned in vessels surrounding the green figure. It gave the room an eerie glow.

"Hello, sister."

She turned slowly to face him. "Tolth, so good to see you." She smiled malevolently.

"You know why I am here," he stated. "Where is she?"

"I have no idea what you mean," she purred.

"Did you kill her?"

"No." She placed her hands on her hips defensively.

"Did you kill Azahleah, too?"

"Tolth, I have not killed anyone." She moved closer to him.

He held out a hand to stop her. "No. I want to know what you did."

"No more than you. Where is Ostram?"

"You know how he is. He might be in the swamps with his furry little creatures." Tolth acted smugly.

"You hid him!" Eryx screamed. "You and the others made a plan against me and hid him from me."

"We did no such thing." Before he could say another word, Eryx blasted him with a fire bolt.

Tolth reeled back into a pillar. "So, this is what happened to the others." Tolth got up.

Eryx took aim again. "They were fools for following you."

Tolth launched a block in her direction. She deflected it, but before she had time to counter, Tolth was in front of her with a tight grip around her throat. He lifted her above his head. "I want you to stop this madness."

"Too late." Eryx brandished a sword and jammed it into Tolth.

Luckily, he shifted enough to keep the strike from being lethal. It stuck in his shoulder. Tolth tossed Eryx down and pulled the sword out. "You leave me no choice."

Eryx created a storm. It lifted Tolth off the ground and slammed him against the temple wall. "And now, you will pay for your choice." She threw a large stone at him. It buried him in a mound of rubble. When he rose up, she stabbed him again. This time, the blade found its mark in his abdomen.

Tolth doubled over. He struck her with the back of his hand. She stood firm. He punched her flush in the face. She remained standing. Tolth grabbed her by the shoulders.

Eryx laughed. "It is over." She punched him and he toppled over.

"You are right," he muttered through blood stained lips.

Flames formed at her feet. Eryx looked confused and then shocked.

Tolth struggled to his feet as Eryx's body burned. "What have you done?" she screamed. The fire did not burn her soul but was destroying the human-like casing that was her body.

Ostram made his appearance from behind her statue. He was chanting aloud.

"I am sorry, sister," Tolth said. "I had to keep you busy long enough for the curse to begin."

"No!" she screamed. Her form, both human and celestial, was bursting into flame.

"Goodbye, Eryx," Tolth said. "I did love you, my sister."

"This is not the en…" Eryx was gone.

Ostram and Tolth gave each other solemn glances.

"Thank you, brother."

Ostram helped himself down from the base of the sculpture. "She is correct, you know. She is not dead."

"I know," Tolth said as he kicked the ashes, all that was left of her corporeal form. The wounds from his fight with her began to heal.

"She only has to find a willing vessel to sacrifice him or herself in her name."

"That may take years."

"Yes, or it may take a day."

"Now, it is my turn to prepare my gift," Tolth said.

"What are your plans?"

Tolth looked at his brother. "I will tell you when I return. Your role here is not yet finished."

"Go and do what you must. Our course is set and the path of peace for Seras will be in your hands."

Chapter Eighteen

"Are you sure I need a phone?" Marcus asked as he and Julie walked into a local cell phone store.

"Yes!" she said loudly. "I told you. I can't just keep popping in and out. It's just not right. Plus, what if I need to get a hold of you for something?" She led him in the direction of the newer phones.

"I've survived on Earth without a phone for three years; what makes you think I need one now?"

"You've survived by cheating."

"May I help you?" a sales clerk asked.

"Oh, no, thank you," Marcus started.

"Yes, he needs a phone. What'cha got?" Julie took over, nudging him out of the way.

The sales clerk began to herd them over to the newest phones. "Please follow me."

"Wait, what about that one?" He pointed to the older, cheaper models.

Julie slapped her forehead with her palm. "Are you kidding?"

"What's wrong with them?" he laughed a little over her protest.

"Um, everything. They're old and nobody uses them anymore."

The sales clerk agreed, nodding her head vigorously.

"But what do I really need it for? I don't need anything fancy. I just need something to answer a call every once in a while."

"Do you need to research anything online?" the salesperson asked.

"Nope," Marcus responded.

"Mr. C.," Julie moaned, "you can't buy a cheap phone. That's embarrassing."

The sales clerk watched the two bicker back and forth over the phone issue.

Marcus raised his hands in the air at shoulder height in protest. "Julie, I don't need to spend a lot of money on something I barely use," he argued.

"Well, I might claim not to know you if you get one of those plastic looking things." She dropped her shoulders and lifted her chin toward the ceiling.

"I can live with that," Marcus joked. When she looked at him with a pretend scowl, he winked.

Then Julie gave him another evil glare and growled.

Two hours later, the two of them arrived at Marcus's apartment. He was carrying an oversized television box. Julie carried a small plastic bag containing his new phone. She swung it merrily back and forth.

"Huh?" Julie asked as she walked through the door.

"I said, 'I hope you're happy'," he said, turning his head to her as he sat the clumsy box on the footstool.

"I am!" Her smile was translucent. "I still think you could've gotten a better phone, but this one isn't bad." She plopped on the couch, opened the box, and pulled out the new purchase.

"I'm glad you approve. You know you're going to have to set it up and teach me how to use it."

"Done."

"What do you mean, 'done'?"

"I just put my number in your phone." She held it up and shook it victoriously.

He stared at her with a look of hindrance.

"What?" she giggled.

"You should be happy. You got what you wanted. I have a phone and a T.V. and you didn't spend any money." He winked at her as he walked to the kitchen to get a butter knife to cut the tape on the box.

"Oh please, you get paid a ton of money, and you haven't spent any of it."

"I don't make a ton of money," he objected. "What am I supposed to do with this thing?" He picked up the television set.

"Oh geesh, you don't have a stand." She twisted her face. "Oops," she said, shrugging. "I guess you should've bought one of those while we were out too."

"Great." He put the television on the floor against the largest wall.

"And, I didn't mean you make a ton of money. I meant that you have been making a lot of money, and other than food and rent, you haven't spent it on anything. So, you have a lot to spend."

"Uh-huh." Marcus smirked. "Now show me how to use this thing." He sat down beside her and let Julie be the teacher for once in their relationship.

~ * ~

"Okay, why are you in a hurry to get to Seras?" Julie asked when Marcus opened the door the next day. "I'm kinda sorry I taught you how to send a text."

"I thought you'd be impressed," he answered, very pleased with himself.

"Ha! Except I was counting on sleeping in this morning." She sat on the couch and began playing with Shakespeare.

"You'll be glad I woke you up." He handed her a cup of chocolate milk.

"Is this supposed to make it better?" She took a long drink.

"Yes." He held out his hand and she took it. He helped her off the couch.

"Okay, what's the rush?"

"You'll see when we get there." He led her to the basement. She gave him a suspicious look, sliding her mouth to one side of her face. "Trust me," he said with a smile.

"I've heard that before," she answered. Julie followed him into the basement and watched as he performed the ritual of igniting the Elders' symbol, stepping into the flame, and then lighting Vestus's gift. "Wait." She stopped him as he started to quickly snatch his hand away from the glow.

"What?"

"Well, if I understand what Redderick has been telling me, the time slower down thingy shouldn't affect you."

"Really?"

"Or me. Watch." She thrust her hand into the emerald light. She waved it up and down, and around and around. "See? We aren't affected."

"How is that possible?" Marcus gave her a confused look. "No one ever told me that."

"I've gotten to teach you twice this weekend." She bobbed her head side to side in celebration. You and I are part of the Elders' gifts. We are immune, I guess. It's all part of some big plan. I don't get it all, but I thought I understood that part."

"Interesting. I'll ask Freya if she knew about this."

"Okay, we can go now." She grabbed his hand and the two walked into the fiery portal.

After they came out of the other side, Julie let go of his hand. That was his sign to grab his clothes, quickly get dressed and get out of his cabin. All of which he did.

When Julie came out of the door, her eyes opened wide at the spectacle in front of her. "What in the world?" she squealed.

Even though night was creeping through the sky, Allon was lit up with large cauldrons of various size, dazzling, colorful paper baskets hung from ropes strung all over the town, pinwheels of sparkling lights twirling in spectacular displays, and festive streamers and ribbons as far as they both could see.

"I knew you would like it." Marcus took it all in. "I popped in last night and saw what they were doing."

"Wait, you came back without me?" She frowned. "And, what are they doing?"

"I only came back without you because I thought it was about this time," he started to explain. "This is our...I guess you would call it our birthday celebration."

She gave him the look of puzzlement. "Huh? My birthday is in June."

"Not ours." He waved his finger to her and him. "Our birthdays." He gestured toward the large group of Allon's residents congregating in the middle of the party. "You see, the people of Seras do not celebrate individual birthdays. We all share a single day to honor the year of our births. It's called the Feast of Tempora."

"I don't get it."

He paused for a moment. "Okay, your birthday is in June. What if instead of celebrating the actual day you just celebrated it at the start of the year?"

"Like on New Year's?"

"Exactly."

"So everyone has the same birthday?"

"Kind of. We don't know the day or the month. We don't have names for days or months, but we all celebrate our years at the time of the great harvest, Tempora."

"So you don't know your birth date at all?"

"No."

"But you know how old you are?"

"I know that this will be my thirty-second Tempora."

"Wow." It was a quiet, awestruck response. Marcus waited for more as she processed the information until finally she said, "Cool!"

"Come on." He started walking toward the middle of the party.

"Wait." She slowed down her pace. "How did you know to check?"

"That's easy. I have it narrowed down to four times a year that it could be. It changes because we come and go, slowing Earth's time and such, but time figures away to make up for it. The time seems to coincide with Earth's equinoxes during the four seasons."

"That's really cool." Julie puckered her lips and nodded her head in approval, then she picked up the pace and the two joined the people of Allon.

Argos met them with drinks. "Welcome, Julie. I am so glad you could be here this year." Argos clasped his elbow around Marcus's elbow and they patted each other's shoulder with their free hand.

"Where was I last time?"

Argos paused as if he wasn't sure what to say.

"It was last summer for you. When you didn't--"

"Oh," she said. "Never mind."

"We didn't celebrate much anyway. It was too soon after Callista's death."

Marcus and Julie looked at each other.

"I'm sorry to bring it up," the commander said.

"Thank you," Julie said. "It wasn't that, though. Do you realize that you are talking different?"

He laughed. "You and Marcus must be rubbing off on me."

Marcus winked at her. Julie smiled almost embarrassed. "Can I go find Seren and Otta?" she asked.

"Of course. You don't need to ask," Marcus answered.

"Seren was by the food. She wanted to be first in line," Argos said with a hint of humor.

Julie skipped away to find her Hemoor friends.

"I've heard you are in charge of the Callistan Tower," Marcus remarked. "How is it coming along?"

"Very well. I have had great help and they have worked to honor her with their dedication to the project," Argos said. The two men sat at a table.

"I am glad to hear that. You have spent a lot of time there."

"As have my sons and my troop. Seren and Otta spend a great deal of time there too."

"Callista would be pleased."

Argos laughed. "We know better. Callista would make fun of us and call us lodear lovers," he said.

Marcus threw back his head in laughter. "Very true." When he finished he said, "I need to take Julie to see it when you are finished."

"I would be honored. Speaking of Julie and Callista, has she been to Callista's site?"

"No. I mentioned it once, but she refused. I have to wait until she is ready." The two warriors finished their drinks.

"Another?" Argos offered as he rose out of his seat.

"Soon. I will visit Freya and a few others first."

"I am glad you brought her." He motioned to Julie dancing with Seren and Otta. "They needed this. The town needed it also."

"Julie needed it too."

Argos wandered away and Marcus found Freya, who was sitting watching the celebration in self-reserve.

"You are too young to not participate in fun every once in a while," he teased his sister as he took a seat next to her.

"That is what I told her," Pertheus said, coming up from behind the pair with two drinks in his hands.

"How are you, my friend?" Marcus accepted the drink from the commander of the foot soldiers. The sounds of children running and laughing echocd through the streets.

"I am doing well. My men are crisp and ready for action," Pertheus said, taking a chug from the wooden mug.

"Let's hope we don't need them anytime soon," Marcus replied. "I want to enjoy the time of peace we have left."

"You know it is coming, though," Freya said.

"Of course, we know," Pertheus answered. "But that doesn't mean we have to spend every waking moment thinking about it." He placed his hands on her shoulders and gently shook her in a playful manner.

Freya slapped his hands away, but a smile crept across her face.

Marcus grinned. Pertheus had done the near impossible and gotten his sister to loosen up.

"Now are you going to dance with me or am I going to have to ask Seren or Otta?"

"Go ask one of them. Marcus and I will stay here and watch as they turn you down."

"Oh, the witch has some bite." Pertheus continued his banter, which made Marcus laugh. Freya relented and accepted Pertheus's hand. He led her to the floor.

Argos and Gwendolyn made way for the two to join the merriment.

Marcus stayed on the periphery, content with watching his companions enjoy each other's company.

~ * ~

Julie moved around the wooden floor. She mimicked the actions of Otta and Seren. Her laughter mixed with theirs. The music changed. The people on the floor circled, women on the outside and the men on the inside. "What are we doing now?"

"Just follow their lead and watch me," Otta said.

The dancers bowed or curtsied. She was across from Julius, the son of Argos. She looked at him with wide eyes. "He looks like he's chiseled outta rock," she whispered.

Otta gave her an approving wink. "I know."

154

He held out his hand. Julie took it. Her hand felt tiny. They raised them in the air.

"Now do this," Otta said as she demonstrated swaying her hips toward her partner, Jakob, Argos's middle son, then back out of the circle. Seren was on the other side of Otta and in front of Edwin.

Julie copied the motion. The entire group walked a full circle and did the swaying thing again before changing partners. Julie curtsied to Julius. "This is fun," she said.

He nodded and smiled. "Thank you. You picked it up pretty quickly."

"Thanks!" Jakob took his place and bowed to her. Julius moved to her right. Julie curtsied again.

As they held hands, Julie decided it must be a family trait. "Your hands are pretty big too."

Jakob thanked her as they walked in a circle. She noticed how the other couples talked and laughed with each other as they danced. He bowed and moved on to Jayna.

"Why aren't they talking to me?" she quietly asked Otta as Edwin moved in front of her and bowed.

"You are the Heart, love."

"Ah, man." She slapped her forehead. "Am I even supposed to be out here?"

"Yes," Otta answered. "They need to get used to you." They marched around and departed with their current partners.

"That's true. I never talk to anyone but you two, Mr. C. and Redderick." She curtsied once again. It was someone she had never seen before. Otta was with Pertheus and Seren was across from Argos.

They clasped hands, but before the couples could finish their waltz-like dance, the music changed. Julie shot Otta and Seren a look.

"It seems they stopped too soon," Otta suggested.

"Just do this," Seren said. She and Argos held both hands up in the air, bringing their bodies closer to one another as they moved in an individual circle, staring intently at each other.

Julie followed. It felt odd being that close to someone she didn't know. "Okay, I've got to stop. I'm sorry," she said to the soldier.

Seren apologized to Argos, "Thank you, sir," and then left to join Julie. Otta thanked Pertheus and went with her two friends.

"I'm sorry," she said as they caught up with her by a table of drinks. "That just weirded me out."

"It does take a while to get used to dancing with strangers or commanders," Otta said.

"But it is all in fun," Seren added.

"I know. I just…this is all still so new to me. And I need to…well, I need to get to know everyone better. Even you two. This is the Feast of Tempora, right? How old are you?"

Seren and Otta looked at each other. Otta shrugged. "We don't know."

Julie stared at them.

"The Hemoor Tribe does not celebrate Tempora," Otta said. "The age of someone didn't matter to us."

"I don't get it."

Otta paused as if to think about how to explain it to her. "Hemoor women never took mates or husbands like other tribes of people did or do. When it was our time to reproduce, we took the strongest or smartest of the slaves."

"Wait, now I'm really confused. You took male slaves to reproduce with? No husbands, no love, or anything like that?"

"No. So when we were born, we just simply were. We were raised by the woman who bore us and then we were put into a unit as soon as we could walk and carry a weapon. There was never a celebration of life, we just were."

"You didn't have mothers?"

"No, we had commanders. And we didn't care how old anyone was, or the person we chose to reproduce with. Age was never a factor."

"Have you…you know, reproduced?" Julie asked, taking a drink to hide her blushed face.

"No, my time never came. The Skorei arrived first."

"Oh, yeah, sorry about that." Then she looked at Seren for an answer.

"I was not a true Hemoor. I was discovered by Heilshorn, Argos, and Callista after my village was destroyed."

"Oh, gosh." Julie closed her eyes and tightened her lips. "I am so sorry. You must hate me for bringing up all of these bad memories."

"No. You are the Heart. I feel honored to be able to share with you." Otta held out her mug to Julie.

"As do I," Seren agreed.

Julie tapped it to signal 'cheers.' Otta looked at her strangely. "Um, it's something we do to…it's," she paused. "Something we do." She shrugged. "So if you don't celebrate birthdays why are you celebrating now?"

"That's easy," Otta started then both she and Seren finished, "We love a good party." The three girls laughed.

Seren took her by the hand. "Are you ready to go back out there?"

Julie's eyes glanced at Mr. Campbell, who was sitting off to the side watching the party. "I am, but let me go talk to Mr. C. first."

Seren released her hand and began to run off with Otta. Julie started walking toward Mr. Campbell. Before they made it to the floor, Erayna, the small Evandell brunette interrupted Gwendolyn and Argos.

"It is time," the sister of the one Julie only knew as the late Alanas said to Gwendolyn.

Argos, Gwendolyn, and Erayna scurried off of the dance floor.

Julie quickened her pace to her teacher. "Is this part of the celebration?"

He was already standing. "No, much bigger than that." He had a smile on his face that made her relax. "Come with me." Mr. Campbell took her by the hand and followed the crowd past the center of town, not far from his cabin. "Where are we going?"

"You'll see." They sifted through the multitude of villagers clamoring around the front door and wood framed window of a similar but homier cottage.

The sounds of pain erupted from the room. A woman was screaming. Julie stopped with a fearful look. She grabbed him by the arm. "What is going on?"

"Laila is giving birth," he said, at almost the same time, Griffus opened the door.

The hulking features of Griffus had softened. In his large arms he held his two newborn children.

Their cries were heard over the admiring audience.

"Twins!" Griffus called out. "This one is a boy." He bounced his right arm proudly. "I will name him Tuco. The word for 'brave.' May he grow to be strong and fearless."

The crowd applauded.

"Why is he purple?" she whispered to Mr. Campbell.

"That's the way newborn babies come out," he explained as Griffus prepared to introduce his second child.

He looks like a Muppet.

Griffus adjusted his left arm for all to see. "This is my daughter. I will name her Beahel. The word for 'river' in the old language. For her, love will flow through our hearts like her name."

The crowd applauded.

"Did you know this was going to happen?" Julie asked as a tear rolled from her cheek.

"No. I knew she was due, but I didn't know it would be tonight." He looked at her. "Are you crying?"

"Shut up." She playfully poked him in the ribs with her elbow.

Chapter Nineteen

"Come," a voice in the dark said.

Julie woke up with a jerk. She rubbed the sleep out of her eyes, once she focused on her early morning guest. "Charlena, what are you doing?"

"Master Redderick wants to see you now," the sandy-haired woman said. Her voice was soft and husky. She handed Julie a fur cloak.

"Seriously?" she muttered, snatching the wrap hurriedly and tossing the blanket off of her.

The morning rain kept the village clouded in gray. Julie followed Charlena quickly to Redderick's tent.

"Not much of a talker, are ya?" Julie tried to joke with the immortal's servant. The girl walked briskly without responding.

The two girls entered Redderick's tent.

"Ah, my child, you look well."

Great, Julie thought. *He's using his annoying sing-song voice.* She shook off the wetness and moved close to the fire he had warming up the quarters. "Why did you wake me up so early?"

"I wanted to get a start on your lesson before you left, my dear."

Julie rubbed her face trying to wake up. "You could have asked me last night. Wait, you weren't even there last night. Why?"

"Tempora is for the people of Seras and the village of Allon. I did not want to interfere."

He sat beside her and placed his hand on her knee. She stiffened in surprise. "I don't think they would've cared. Everyone was there."

He studied her as she spoke. "I suppose you are right. But I would have rather stayed here with my own company."

Oh gross, she thought, looking at the five women lounging in the back of the room. "I almost forgot."

"I hope you had an enjoyable evening."

"I did. The Tempora was a lot of fun. And Griffus and Laila had twins last night."

"So they did." Redderick nodded in approval then changed the topic. "Now where were we?"

"Tolth and Ostram beat Eryx and banished her from Seras," Julie answered.

"Indeed," he responded. "I am pleased with how well you are remembering."

"So what happened to Eryx?" she asked. "Did she eventually die?"

Redderick shifted. "No, my child, I am afraid she found one that sacrificed herself in her name, and she is regaining her strength through her new vessel."

"What?" Julie shouted and stood. "When, how…who?" She stomped around the room. "Why hasn't she been stopped?"

He chuckled. "Julie, that is why we are here, to stop Eryx and her plans." He got up to calm her down. "I will need you to sit down so I can help you understand."

"Fine," she huffed and returned to her seat.

"It happened a little over seventeen years ago. It is called the Avinimere, or Ripple in Time. When it happened here, you were born." He stopped and stared at her.

She looked at him in disgust. "What are you talking about?"

"You are making me get ahead of myself," Redderick laughed.

"It's not funny," Julie said.

"No, my dear, it's not. But let me start with Lord Tolth. Then everything will make perfect sense."

"Well, get started," she said, "because I am going crazy. How am I supposed to figure out what all of this means if I don't have all of the information I need? I mean, seriously! Do you know how hard all of this is to believe? So let me hear it."

The immortal rubbed his cheek. Seeing her resolve, he began telling her the story. "Good. Let me start with a girl." He looked admiringly at Julie. "A girl a little older than yourself."

Through a rugged landscape, remote and steep with lines of stone walls where hundreds of turkeys and llamas roamed, beyond a thick stand of trees revealed a vegetation shroud. The place was known as The Crown of the Jungle; its dense, lush rainforest obscured by the ragged, jutting walls of a misty canyon. A narrow trail led down the canyon into the green, flora canopy.

As dusk settled, a family slowly and quietly moved through the narrow streets of the village while a huge crowd thronged around a massive square. At the end of the solemn procession, a young woman rode in a golden litter atop the shoulders of six men.

As the girl got nearer to the square, the villagers became excited, shouting and making clamorous noise as they ran up and down the street. The noise grew rowdy and sharp with excitement and violence. Two lit pyres stood on the far end of the square. The faces of her family were somber. They spoke near silent prayers.

The crowd turned to face the temple perched on a hill. Just beyond the pyres stood the isolated and austere Temple of The Pale Jaguar.

The pyramid stood forty feet in height with eleven levels. Stairs carved into the shape of scaled serpents led to the eighth level where a platform was staged. Chiseled panthers guarded the gateway and a caldron sat over the entrance of the temple, which was formed in the likeness of the open jaws of a great cat. The pyramid was in poor condition and dirty from lack of care.

A hooded priest greeted the brigade and helped the woman from the litter while a dozen other hooded priests restrained her family. A hooded priest walked her to the first step. Dutifully, the young woman looked back at her family, who were crying in vain. The flames of the pyres leaped into the night with terrible crackling, lighting up half-charred figures of men in their luring glow. The dead men's necks had been snapped like burning wood and their heads fell against one shoulder, blood residue from the sacrificial letting pooled under their feet. They were sacrificed to begin the ceremony. Each of their bodies had been cut loose from the support beams and hesitated eerily before collapsing into the fire.

The young woman hid her face in her hands, shielding her eyes from the horror. One of the hooded priests took a lit torch and escorted her up the steep temple steps to where a high priest awaited on the first level platform.

The deistic man was dressed in white with a plated gold belt and headdress. He had a silver necklace fashioned in the form of the large jungle cat. He spoke to the girl in an ancient language. "The temple is alive with His presence," he said slowly almost methodically. "Your people need you to be his bride.

She looked down from the platform to her family below. The crowd around them were less subdued, chanting enthusiastically. "My family knows they will never see me again," she said to him in revulsion.

"You are a brave woman, Isa." The priest spoke nobly with a hint of an edge.

"We both know why I have been chosen," she nearly spat.

"It is not too late to change your mind. I can always pick a replacement," he teased.

"I would rather die."

"Very well. Follow me." He offered his hand, which she refused. "Consider yourself very lucky." The two moved up the stairs to the temple entrance. "The temple has been quiet for decades," he said as

he used his staff to move the branches of the entwined trees that guarded the temple. "The gods have finally asked for a true sacrifice."

"What about the others whom you have sacrificed in the name of the Pale Jaguar?" she asked, afraid to know the answer.

"My discretion, my pleasure." His lips curled like the vegetation over the crevices. "It served my purpose."

Isa began to weep at the hopelessness of her position.

"Last chance, Isa. Surely being with me would be better than this."

"No," she defied him.

He turned to the masses and held up his staff with both hands over his head. The chanting grew. "The Pale Jaguar requests a bride. Isa is that bride." The crowd erupted. Her family sobbed.

He led her through the rounded entrance, which was designed to look like fanged jaws. It opened to a wet, dark, tubular passage. It was dirty with plant life and blood. Their footsteps on the broken tiled floor echoed in synchronicity with the loud dripping from the ceiling.

The priest occasionally looked back to his latest victim. Isa followed in silence. They reached an arch in the hall of the small chamber. A bright light lit by a shaft of moonlight shone on the altar.

"Lie down. This will all be over soon," he said with a grim smile.

"Why should I believe you?"

"Your family and your village are depending on you. You would hate to disappoint them." Then he commanded, "Lie down."

Hesitantly, yet proudly, she moved toward the stone altar, climbed up the three carved steps, and lay down, staring up at the moss covered rocks above her, whispering a continuous prayer to one of their gods of their village.

The High Priest took great pleasure inspecting her body. "Such a waste." He fanned her with a big leafy branch and then waved incense over her before tearing her frock, exposing her light brown chest.

She gasped in modesty. *"Chasca, save me!"* She winced as he drew a large, curved knife with a golden blade and jewel encrusted handle and began to drag the razor-edge between her breasts and down her sternum drawing a stream of blood. Isa screamed as the priest raised the decorated knife over his head and plunged it toward her heart.

Isa woke on the floor of a massive, domed room with a golden ceiling and whitewashed stone tiled floor. She was wearing a sheer blue gown with a pure white rope around her waist for a belt. Golden bracelets adorned her wrists and silver and gold draped her elegant neck. The knife cut down her chest was gone. On one end of the room was a clean, pearly altar that only bore a slight resemblance to the one she was just killed on.

"Am I dead?" She began walking down a straight fifty-foot long hallway. There were mosaics of animals in blue, red, orange, and yellow stones. Shafts of sunlight shone down through honeycombed skylights. A white archway greeted her at the end of the hall. Isa looked over a vast sea of blue water over a starlit open sky. A rumbling noise surrounded her. The water parted. She stood in amazement as crystal columns rose four wide about ten feet apart in two rows. In the distance, a marble platform ascended from the depths.

The platform had four wide steps with two golden cauldrons fully ignited at the top. A marble recliner sat in the middle of the platform. Sprawled upon the royal seat was a white jaguar.

"Manco Cápac, it is you…"

The giant jaguar leaped off of its perch and roared loud enough to shake the place where Isa was standing. Then from the waters rose a golden brick walkway that led from the arched entryway to the magnificent sanctuary.

Isa began her careful walk across the bridge. Ribbons of pearly mist swarmed around her as she got closer and closer to the beautiful animal. She politely bowed her head to the large white cat.

It placed a front paw on the top step and then another, by the third step the jaguar was gone and in its place stood a tall, handsome man with violet eyes and long blonde hair. He was wearing a blue cloak over a white sarong. His chest and feet were bare. "I am not Manco Cápac." His voice surrounded her like the pearled mist. "I am Tolth."

"So, this is death?" she asked.

"No, Isa, this is not death. This is the beginning of life for you."

"I do not understand."

"Nor will I take the time to explain much of it to you." He held out his hand for her to take.

When she did, he led her up the stairs to the recliner. His grip was strong, yet tender. He wore one golden bracelet the length of his forearm on both wrists and a chain of gold with a strange design hung from his neck. Tolth asked the wisps of wind, "Is she purified?" Only an odd shrill was his answer. "Then leave us."

Confused, Isa asked, "My lord?"

"No, not you." Tolth turned to her and placed his hands on her face. "Isa, my faithful servant, I ask that you allow me to use you as my vessel to carry my seed from generation to generation until the day of atonement?"

"I do not understand, my lord."

"The choice is yours. I can only ask that you grant me permission, so through you, my people will not be punished for my sins."

"Will I die?"

"No, you will live. You will be my High Priestess and live for many years, and your people will love you."

"Then let it be so," she agreed.

His mouth consumed hers. He moved her toward the recliner and unfastened her gown.

Isa stood naked before Tolth.

He removed his cloak and sarong and eased Isa back to the recliner. "I am Tolth. You are my vessel, and through your line my sins against God and man will be forgiven." Tolth moved over her as Isa closed her eyes.

"Uh, gross. You could've left that part out," Julie said in disgust, stopping the story.

"My apologies," Redderick said and continued his story. "Very well…"

Outside the temple, the villagers fell to their knees as a thunderous earthquake shook the ground under their feet. The temple's foundation rumbled relentlessly, causing dirt and debris to fly in the wake of the upheaval.

Isa woke up on the altar, now clean. The High Priest laid dead. She took his staff and struck the ground with it. The staff shone brightly in her hand and turned to gold. She walked out to face her subjects.

The temple was adorned in white and gold and shone as if freshly painted by the newly risen sun.

The hooded priests of the temple died at the sight of her.

Isa stood before her village in her white garb, round and fully large with child. "I am Isa. Priestess of Tolth. The Chosen Vessel of Tolth." She placed a hand on her stomach. "Keeper of the Temple of Tolth. Never again will this temple be subjected to sacrifices to false needs or wants. Let my words be His words, and let me lead you as He sees fit. Through me, His preparation will be complete."

"So, this Isa girl became Tolth's Chosen One? What happened to her? Why didn't she do whatever I'm supposed to do?" Julie asked.

"I am not finished, yet."

In her thirtieth year as the temple priestess of Tolth, Isa called for her daughter; the daughter given to her by the strange deity of the temple. As she sat in a chair in her chamber area, Isa turned to face her devoted progeny. "Mila, my daughter, it is time for you to take my place as priestess of the temple."

"Why, Mother?" her daughter responded with concern.

"I have lived a good life and it is now your time."

"No, it is not my wish." The beautiful woman rushed to her mother, kneeling at her side.

"But, it is mine. It is time for you to carry on the will of Tolth." She petted her daughter's long dark hair. "Before I depart--"

"Depart!"

"Yes, before I depart, you must do this one thing."

"I do not understand."

"I spoke those same words thirty years ago," Isa consoled her daughter.

"Mother?"

"Mila, I love you. Please do as I say without question." Isa led her daughter to her desk and motioned for her to sit. "I want you to write down the words that I say."

"Yes, mother." Mila sat and flattened out a scroll of parchment. "To my beloved people. There will come a day when we will be overcome by strangers. Do not be afraid. We are to embrace these visitors. Entwine with them in their ways and leave our homes. When this time comes, make preparations to destroy the temple and all of its possessions."

"Mother, no!"

"Mila, it must be done. It is Tolth's wish." Isa continued, "Take with you only that which is necessary to live and keep peace among yourself and the strangers. I do not know when these visitors will come, only that they will. Do not resist. If you do, all in the name of Tolth will be lost." She made sure Mila kept up. "Keep this safe. I do not know when this will happen, but you must promise me that my words will be remembered."

"I will, Mother."

"Now, Mila, it is time." Isa stood and reached out for her daughter.

"Time?"

"Yes, it is time for you to choose a husband and keep our bloodline flowing, and if I am not mistaken, there is a certain young man who would be happy to do so."

"Oh, yes, Mother!" Mila shouted as she hugged her mother and ran off to find her heart's desire.

Isa passed shortly after her daughter's wedding and the birth of a handsome boy. Isa and Mila's descendants reigned over the village as High Priestess or High Priest for over one thousand years until the arrival of the Spaniards in the 1500s.

Then, as instructed in the parchment left by Isa, written by her daughter, Mila, and passed down from generation to generation, when news of strangers arriving from the great ocean and marching through the tropical forest of their homeland reached their ears, the villagers did as they were instructed by their High Priest--toppled their temple and burned the village to the ground. The Spanish explorers took pity on the homeless people and made them guides, slaves, and eventually spouses.

"Okay," Julie said in a confused tone. "Why did you have to tell me this story?"

"You don't understand? My dear, you weren't paying attention," the immortal said. He looked at her and grinned. "I told you this story because, my dear, this is half of the story of your bloodline…the bloodline of Tolth. Through the body of the young virgin, Isa, it spread upwards from the South American jungles to the prairies and grasslands of the southwest of North America until a young Gabriela Mendes married a local farm boy, Bobby Franklin, who took a job in a factory and eventually moved his family to a small rural town in Sunset, Ohio."

"Oh, my gosh!"

Chapter Twenty

"Are you coming?" Julie's dad asked as he and her mother began heading down the stairs.

Julie moaned. Saturday mornings were not her best time. "Where?" she answered, lifting her head from the pillow.

Her father stopped. "Really?"

"What?"

"Julie, I've been planning this day for over a year. Where have you been?" Her father's face showed a look of disappointment.

"I'm just kidding," she lied trying to hide the fact that she had been so busy in Seras that she forgot about, "the Chocolate Festival, of course."

Phillip twisted his face in doubt. "Then let's hurry up."

Julie hopped out of bed, closed the door to wiggle into a pair of denim jean shorts and change her shirt. She quickly slid on her running shoes and raced down the stairs.

Once they arrived in town, Julie was rethinking her choice of wearing shorts. The lawn of the town square was still damp with dew. She hoped the spring sun would burn off the chill before too long.

"Are your friends going to be here?" Julie's mother asked as her father left them to help set up booths, rope off areas, and make sure vendors were ready for the anticipated crowd.

"I know Claire won't be. She has a meet today. Jimmy will probably go watch her run."

"That's sweet."

Julie noticed her mother's face. "What?"

"Nothing," her mother answered.

"Come on, let me hear it. You think they are too serious too soon, or you think they are too young to be so committed to each other like they are?"

"Actually, neither. I was wondering who has been occupying your time."

Julie contorted her face. "What? Nobody," she snorted.

"Honey, you're never around, and even when you are, you aren't here. I'm just wondering why we haven't met him yet. Are you embarrassed by us?"

"No, I don't get why you think that. I've just been really...really," she paused longer, "really busy."

"Okay, I guess I have to believe you."

The festival looked like a carnival. Her father had banners hung, a large stage, and vendor tents everywhere. The only thing missing was the crowd. It was sparse. A few hundred people moved through the square during the course of the afternoon.

"Spring is so hard to predict." Julie heard her father talking to his former high school classmate, the mayor.

"Yeah, this weather isn't helping," the mayor said.

"First year problems," Phillip shrugged. "Every year will get bigger and better."

"Maybe the crowning of the queens will help a little."

The mini-ceremony to name the queens was slightly more populated than the earlier draws. Her dad, the mayor, and Mr. Frye served as judges. A girl with long jet-black hair won the title of queen in the senior division and a little curly-haired blonde, named Maggie, won the crown in the junior division. The other contestants applauded along with family members and friends.

~ * ~

Julie drove her mother's car up Claire's driveway to her best friend's split-level ranch. Claire was sitting on the porch waiting to be picked up.

"How did you do this weekend?" Julie asked Claire as she climbed into the passenger seat.

"Good! Mr. Langston said my times are coming down. I wish you would've come out for the team."

"Me too! You are doing so great!" Julie headed back down the drive toward the main road.

"We have our last dual of the year on Tuesday. Can you make it?"

"Of course I will. What time does it start?" Julie asked.

"Cool! I think it starts at five. Coach Langston told me I'm running the four hundred dash and the four by four relay."

"Wow! You really must be doing great. I've heard Langston tell people the four hundred is the toughest race in track."

"He wasn't lying. I'm so nervous. Having my best friend there will make it so much better," Claire said.

"Yay!" Julie cheered.

Claire smiled and then sat back as Julie drove to school. "I can't believe how fast this year has gone."

"It has, hasn't it? I can't believe finals are less than a month away."

"It doesn't seem like we hang out as much as we used to." Claire's smile turned to more of a pout.

"I know. It's my fault. I think this year has been so hectic. Classes have been crazy, cheer was crazy, then basketball and you have track." Julie shrugged. "I hate it."

"Me too."

Julie pulled into the school drive and found a parking space. "It'll get better. Summer is coming."

"Yeah, with more cheer practices and basketball camps and summer track." Claire frowned.

"Stop. We'll be okay." Julie comforted her friend. They walked into the building and hugged before going their separate ways. Claire went to find Jimmy and Julie went to her locker.

Julie felt guilty. After school, she and Mr. Campbell made their way to Seras to practice her sword fighting skills.

Julie began swinging wildly with overhead chopping motions and uncontrolled baseball strikes.

"Whoa, wait!" Mr. Campbell said, stopping her. "What are you doing?"

"Nothing, why?"

"Well, besides the long periods of silence and a half dozen 'nothings' since we got here, you are handling your sword like a maniac."

"Oh, great!" Julie screamed. "Now I can't even do this right." She threw her sword down and stormed away from him.

"Hey, I never said that."

"You just did! You said I was swinging my sword like a maniac." She wanted to cry but held strong.

"I know what I said, Julie. I just want to know what's going on."

"Never mind," she huffed.

"No, I'm not going to let you 'never mind' me now. Tell me what's wrong."

"Fine," she said loudly. "I'm so freaking busy that I haven't been able to hang out with my friends, spend time with my family, or do anything fun. Claire is running track right now, and I haven't seen her compete all spring. Heck, school is over in a month, and I have nothing to show for it."

"What does that mean?"

"I haven't done anything. I haven't made any new friends. I haven't accomplished any goals. I haven't even dated a whole lot. Heck, I haven't even been asked to prom."

"Julie, I'm sorry. I just wanted to make sure--"

"I know. Forget it. I told you it was nothing." She moved to a fallen tree and sat down in frustration.

"It's not nothing." He sat beside her.

"Yes, it is. This is what I have to do."

"But it doesn't have to consume your life."

"Since when doesn't it have to consume my life?" Julie argued. "Because you brought me here, and you don't want me to end up like Callista…" She stopped. Her eyes showed that she said that without thinking about what was coming out of her mouth. "Oh, my God! I didn't mean to say that."

"No, I'm glad you did. It's about time we got that in the open."

"Yep, well, that's me being all openy. Yes, I know that is not a word."

"You're right."

Julie looked at him and anger began to boil up inside of her. She got up and walked away.

Her teacher followed her. "That is not a word, but you're also right, I don't want you to end up like Callista. Every time we practice, you have to be perfect. If you miss a block, it could be your last. If you miss an attack, it could be your last."

"Why are you saying that?" Her voice came out in a gravelly hiss.

"Because I don't want you to die." It sounded almost like a plea.

"Good! Because I'm not crazy about the idea either."

"Then you have to take this seriously."

"I am!" she screamed. "Can't you see that I am?"

"Then you can't be distracted."

"Okay, I don't like how this is going. I just told you I was feeling bad about not hanging out with Claire, and you jump all over me." Julie sat down on the cool morning grass still slightly damp with the previous night's dew.

"Julie, I…" Mr. Campbell stammered.

"Forget it. Just take me home."

He gave her a defeated look.

"I'm serious. Take me home." She rolled far enough over to push herself off the ground. When she stood, she wiped her hands off on her skirt and looked at him with insolence.

"Okay, come on." He led her to the horses.

Now that she was becoming a much better rider, she was happy that she didn't have to depend on his help. She rode ahead of him so she could avoid talking to him or seeing the hurt on his face.

When they got to the cabin, they were met by Redderick Bobo.

"Julie, may I have a word with you?" the immortal asked.

"Not now; I'm a little busy." Julie walked past him into the cabin. Mr. Campbell followed her in, as did Redderick.

"I insist you stay," Redderick said.

"Sorry about that," Julie snapped.

"We have to go," Mr. Campbell said apologetically.

The immortal grabbed her by the arm. "Let me go," Julie yelled at him, whipping her arm away but not breaking the man's grip.

"Let her go," Marcus said loudly.

The immortal paused for a second before saying, "No, I have to--"

"Let her go," Mr. Campbell repeated through clenched teeth. Julie had never seen him angry like that before.

Redderick let his hand relax.

Julie pulled away and rubbed her triceps area. She looked at both men.

"I need her to stay," Redderick said, though not as forcefully as he was with her.

She couldn't decide what to do.

"Julie, you can go. I will handle this," Mr. Campbell said to her almost as if Redderick wasn't there.

"Fine. Whatever." She lit the portal and went through alone.

~ * ~

"I sense you have a problem with me," Redderick said, his voice pleasantly fake.

"You do not understand what she is going through. We have done nothing but push her this entire year," Marcus answered.

"We need her to be ready. You prepare her physically and I prepare her mentally. When we are finished with her, Queen Pallanex will not be able to defeat her."

Marcus turned away from him in frustration then turned back to face Redderick. "Let me face Queen Pallanex. I killed her once, I can kill her again, and this time I will make sure she doesn't come back."

"If only it were that easy," the immortal said. "She is more powerful now than ever before." He sat on Marcus's bed. "And, I'm afraid she is getting more powerful by the day."

"Why does it have to be Julie?"

"It was not my choice. This is part of Tolth's plan."

Marcus blew out a sigh of defeat. "Give her a few days without your cursed stories or my training so that she can enjoy the last few weeks of school, and I promise I will bring her back."

"You are taking a chance that we have that kind of time," Redderick stated, getting up from his seat.

"What if we don't?" he had to ask.

"The end of Seras," Redderick said. "The end of Earth." He shrugged sarcastically. "The end of our worlds and possibly beyond."

Chapter Twenty-one

Julie handed five dollars to a lady sitting in a chair who gave her a ticket and said "Thank you."

"Thank you," Julie answered back, shoving the ticket in her jean shorts pocket.

"You know, you could be here for free," a voice behind her said. She turned quickly to see the smiling face of Mr. Langston.

"Hi, Mr. Langston," she said, shaking her head back and forth.

"I'm serious. You would make a great track athlete." He caught up with her and tapped her on the arm with a rolled up program.

"How do you know?" she asked. Her green Cedar Creek t-shirt matched his green polo shirt with yellow sleeves and a black and white penguin emblem on his chest. His green ball cap had "Cedar Creek Track and Field" emblazoned on the front.

"Coaching intuition. Mr. Campbell has told me how hard you work in the weight room, and I've watched you play basketball and cheer. You could be a great addition to the team." He led her to the giant tent set up under the bleachers.

"Thanks. I'll think about it for next year."

"I'll hold you to that." He turned to the athletes sitting in the tent. "Get out there and support your teammates."

Claire hopped up from the ground where she had her bag placed, getting ready for the meet to start. "Oh, I can't believe you made it," she shrieked and gave Julie a hug.

"When do you run?"

"Not for a while. The four by two is my first race, and it starts at noon."

"Cool."

"In fact, I need to go do handoffs as soon as the rest of my team gets out of the restroom."

"What else are you running today?"

"The four by two, the four hundred, and the four by four," she answered. "It's an easy day today, usually Coach has me running the two hundred dash too, but he really wanted to see the four by four run fresh."

"Yeah, I really don't know what that means," Julie joked.

"I know. I'll explain it later."

Three of Claire's teammates approached. Julie knew two of them, so they all exchanged hugs.

Claire had a green baton in her hand and flashed it in front of their eyes. "Coach says we need to practice. He is waiting on the far side of the track." The girls grabbed their spikes and started to leave. "Are you going to wait here?" she asked Julie.

"No, I'll either be in the stands or I might walk around and check out the field events."

"Jimmy is over at the high jump. Girls are jumping first, but he likes to go over early and check things out."

"Okay, thanks. Good luck!" They hugged again and Claire jogged away.

Julie walked out from under the bleachers. The sun was already warming the air. It was going to be a hot day. She walked around the field events, watched a couple of the female throwers working on their spin for the discus throw, a couple of boys throwing the shot put, two Cedar Creek boys long jumping, two other boys pole vaulting, and Jimmy helping two girls over by the high jump area. She darted across the track toward him. It was good to see a familiar face. "Hey!"

"Hi, what are you doing here?" he asked, the sun already starting to leave its mark on his thinning forehead. "Have you seen Claire-bear, yet?"

"I have. She's doing handoffs somewhere." Julie looked around.

"Oh, over there, on the back stretch." Jimmy pointed at a spot on the opposite end of the track from where they were. "Coach L. is a stickler for handoffs."

"It's like a three-ring circus here," she said.

Jimmy laughed. "I know, right? There's something for everyone."

"What are you doing?" she asked.

"I'm helping them." He pointed his thumb at two Cedar Creek girls huddled together in the corner of the high jump apron. "We don't have a high jump coach, so Coach Langston has me help mark their steps and stuff."

Julie watched Jimmy coach the two girls' high jumps. When they finished, Julie excused herself to go sit in the stands as close to the finish line as she could. She watched Claire run her first race, the four by two hundred relay, it was the fourth race of the day, following the four by eight hundred relay, the one hundred meter hurdles, and the one hundred meter dash. Each girl had to run two hundred meters or half the distance around the track. When Claire, who was the final leg of the relay, the anchor, got the baton, Cedar Creek was in third place. The whole crowd stood up as the eight teams headed for the finish line. Claire, with her long legs, closed in on the two runners in front of her, passed one girl, and narrowly missed catching the first-place girl.

Claire found Julie shortly afterward. She still looked mad. "I can't believe I didn't catch her."

"You did so good!"

"Thanks. We ran our best time of the year, but still." Claire plopped down beside her.

The two cheered for Claire's teammates in the sixteen hundred run. "I've gotta go get ready for the four hundred, it comes after the four by one," Claire said.

"Good luck!"

Claire left, and Julie watched both the boys' and girls' four hundred relays. She laughed as she watched Mr. Langston run along the fence line yelling for the anchors to run faster. *He's like a really weird cheerleader*. Mr. Langston moved toward the high jump area to coach Jimmy as Claire lined up in her blocks and took off around the track. By the time Claire got to the home stretch, Julie was standing beside him, joining him as he was jumping up and down, screaming his head off. Claire crossed the line in second place. Julie could see the frustration in her eyes.

"Two races, ugh!" Claire said as she made her way back to Mr. Langston and Julie.

Mr. Langston gave her a supportive hug. "You did great!"

"Yeah, ya did," Jimmy added as he took off his sweatpants to get ready to jump.

"You were awesome!" Julie said. "Oh, my gosh, you killed it."

"I almost had her," Claire said, wiping the sweat from her body.

The two friends watched Coach Langston prepare Jimmy for the high jump. Claire's boyfriend cleared six feet four inches and won first place. From the high jump apron, they were able to watch the rest of the team compete on the track. When it came time for the final race, the four by four hundred relay, Claire and her teammates were closing in on the team in first place. Jimmy and the boys' team had the invitational all wrapped up, but Jimmy was just as excited to anchor the final relay of the day. "It's the best race ever," he said as he left to get warmed up.

Claire, on the other hand, looked nervous.

"You ready?" Julie asked. Claire started moving toward the finish line.

"I am," she answered. "I have to get checked in."

"Good luck."

"Thanks!"

Julie watched as Jimmy anchored his team to an easy victory. Claire's team took their place on the track. When the baton got to Claire, it was her versus the girl who had beaten her in the earlier four hundred race. The two girls battled back and forth down the backstretch. As they turned the corner and headed for the finish, Claire had the look of sheer determination on her face. She passed the girl with less than fifteen meters left and her team won the relay, and even more importantly, her team won the whole meet.

Claire's team cheered and screamed in excitement. Both the girls and boys lined up together for pictures from proud parents. They did a final cheer and began packing up to leave. Julie met Claire at the team camp area.

"That was the coolest thing ever!" Julie hugged her best friend.

"I thought I was going to die," Claire said. "There was no way I was going to let her beat me this time."

"I'm so proud of you." Julie then changed the subject. "I'll see you tonight at prom."

"Yes, I have to get dressed, and Jimmy's mom promised to do my hair. I have so much to do."

"I'm sure you'll look great."

"Thank you so much for coming." The two hugged again and then Julie left to get herself ready. "Pictures at six, right?"

"Yep, see you there," Claire answered.

~ * ~

Julie looked at the big alabaster Italian restaurant. Her prom date, the blond, curly-haired, green-eyed boy named Mike from chemistry, pulled his car to the front door where parent chaperones waited to open doors and valet park the cars for the students. Fathers and a few mothers wore green and yellow tuxedo t-shirts.

She waited for Mike, who was wearing a black suit with a blue bowtie and matching cummerbund that clashed with Julie's sparkly red dress. The miss-matched attire stressed her out, but she held it in.

Inside the restaurant, the large fountain was full of black and white balloons. Soft jazz played throughout the building. Julie handed her ticket to Mr. Frye with a bright smile and excited eyes.

"Well, well, well," a voice said from behind her.

"Hi, Mr. C.," Julie said before turning around.

"Hey, Mr. C." Mr. Campbell stuck out his hand and her date shook it.

"I didn't think they let sophomores in here," Mr. Campbell said.

"Only if you get asked by an upperclassman," Julie responded with a head bob. He was wearing a red shirt, black pants, black shoes and a gold pocket watch. The question of why they match better than her and her date crossed her mind.

"I know," he joked with a wink. "Have a good time, you two."

"Thanks, Mr. C.," they said in unison.

The main ballroom was decorated in a black and white, classic fifties motif. Julie looked at the hanging banner. "It looks like Miss Slovarsky's theme is 'High Society'."

"Oh, my goodness!" Miss Slovarsky shrieked. "You two look fantastic."

Julie hugged the excitable math teacher. "Thank you. I love the theme."

"You do?" Miss Slovarsky asked, holding her by the shoulders.

"Heck yes, Bing, Louis, and…"

"Grace Kelly," both said at the same time.

"Oh, I loved her," Miss Slovarsky said.

"She was gorgeous," Julie added.

"Hey!" Claire waved, catching Julie's attention. She and Jimmy were saving two seats.

Julie hugged Miss Slovarsky a final time. "Make sure you get a picture taken," the teacher advised.

"I will." Julie smiled and led her date toward the table to sit with her best friend. Claire was wearing a pink chiffon dress. Jimmy had a pink tie against a white shirt and black jacket.

"Hi guys," Julie said. She and Claire hugged as Jimmy and Mike shook hands.

"Thank you for coming to the meet today," Claire said in her ear as they embraced.

"Oh, gosh, I loved it. I really want to run track now," Julie said.

Claire clapped. "That would be so much fun!"

They said hello to the other two couples at the round table and took their seats. "You guys rock," Julie told the couple sitting nearest to Claire and Jimmy.

"We're glad it worked out," the guy said, and the group didn't say another word about it.

Julie looked over at Mr. Campbell. He was sitting at a table with Miss Slovarsky and her fiancé and Mr. Langston, Mr. Schultz, and Mr. Frye and their wives. "Poor Mr. Campbell," Julie whispered.

"What?" Claire leaned over and asked.

"Look at him over there, sitting with all of those couples, and he has no one."

"Yeah, I really thought him and Slovarsky were going to hook up," Claire said.

"I remember that," Julie said. "Halloween our freshman year." Julie thought back to that night, the awkward feeling of seeing him as she was dressed like a gothic cheerleader. "I was mortified."

"About him and Slovarsky?" Jimmy broke into the conversation.

Julie laughed. "No, about him seeing me dressed in that outfit." Then she thought about later that night and how he had saved her from that crazy woman in the alley. "I'm going to go grab a soda. Do you guys want anything?"

"I'm good," Claire answered. "How 'bout you?" she asked Jimmy.

"Good here," he said, starting to take off his jacket before Claire stopped him.

"No, we still have pictures."

"Okay," Julie said before walking away. She saw Mr. Campbell getting a drink and snuck behind him. "So what brings you to the bar?"

His body jerked. "Oh, Julie, you scared me."

"Could you be any less convincing?" She rolled her eyes at his attempt to be funny.

"And this is the refreshment area, not a bar."

"Whatever. If we weren't students, this would definitely be the bar. Look, tall chairs that rotate." She sat and demonstrated, swiveling the chair back and forth. "Just because they put pop and stuff on it for us doesn't mean it's not a bar."

He nodded in agreement. "But do you know how many parents would have heart attacks if we called this a bar during prom?"

"True." Julie made a noise through her nose, part laugh and part snort, that made Julie laugh even louder.

"So how did they get here together?" Mr. C. pointed with his chin toward the table she shared with Claire and Jimmy.

"Easy, if you promise not to tell."

"I promise."

"Good. See the other couple?" Julie asked.

"Yes, but I don't know them."

"Chris is a senior, and Anna is a junior. So Chris bought Claire's ticket and Jimmy bought Anna's. So they just switched dates when they got here," Julie explained.

"I see."

"You promised not to tell," she said, making sure he would keep his word.

"I promise."

"Cool. Well, have fun."

"You too."

"I will." She turned on her heels, stuck out her tongue, and rejoined her date and friends for a night of dinner and dancing.

~ * ~

Two weeks later, Julie was in the stands to watch the newest graduating class receive their diplomas. She sat with her parents in the track and football stadium bleachers on the warm May evening.

"Poor Mr. C.," Julie said.

"What's wrong with Mr. Campbell?" Michelle asked.

"He's still behind Mr. Langston in giving kids their diplomas," she answered with a smile.

"I really don't think it's a contest," her father said.

"Not at this rate--he's getting his butt kicked." Julie laughed. Her mom and dad shook their heads.

The crowd waved and clapped for the students as they filed in during the playing of "Pomp and Circumstance." Just like last year, they matched the school colors: the boys wore green robes and the girls wore yellow.

The president of the school board, an older gentleman with just enough hair around his head to look like a victory wreath, spoke first and then introduced Mr. Frye.

Mr. Frye listed all of the graduating seniors' accomplishments during their four years of "terror…I mean high school," he joked. The audience laughed right on cue.

"I love Mr. Frye," Julie said. "He's the best."

After the ceremony, Julie made her way to some of the graduating girls, many of whom were on her basketball team and cheerleading squad. Hugs and tears were shared before the football field eventually emptied.

And, just like last year, Julie found Mr. Campbell and begged to hold off going back to Seras until after the graduation parties were over.

~ * ~

"Welcome back, my dear," Redderick Bobo said as Julie entered his tent. "It has been too long. I have missed you."

"Well, I can't really say the same," she answered.

"I take it that your little break went well."

"Better than you can imagine." Her mind drifted to the merriment of prom night. "Eh, nothing you would understand."

"Probably not. That is best left to you and your Mr. Campbell."

"Yeah," she dragged out slowly. "Already did, and he stayed for most of it." Then she changed the subject. "So you never told me why Isa or Mila didn't do the job as the Heart?"

"They were not the Heart," Bobo said.

"But you said…"

"I was not finished. They were only one part of a bigger story."

"Then finish it." She knew impatience was not the key, but she couldn't help it.

"Gladly."

In the year 375 A.D. in the land of the pharaohs, there was another significant birth. Not significant in the history of the world known as Earth, but significant for the world called Seras.

Eshe was the unwed daughter of a poor Hebrew merchant. In her twentieth year, she went out on an errand for her mother. In the hot, desert sun, Eshe became thirsty. She stopped at a well for a drink.

Looking down, she saw something shining in the water. Eshe tried to maneuver the bucket to scoop up whatever it was. As she adjusted herself on the unsteady rocks, she slipped and fell down the well. When she awoke, Eshe was laying on top of a pearly white altar of marble inside the domed room of Tolth. She looked around at the large golden ceiling and whitewashed tiled floor. She was wearing a sheer white gown with a purple sash as a belt. Bracelets and necklaces of gold and silver decorated her wrists and neck. "I must be in

Heaven," she thought to herself, sad that her foolishness had cost her her life.

On the other side of the room was a long hallway. Mosaics of animals in blue, red, orange, and yellow stones lined the walls. Sunlight shone down through honeycombed skylights. When she got to the end of the hallway, she stood under a white archway. There, Eshe saw an endless sea of blue water over an open, starlit sky. Just as it had done for Isa, a rumbling noise surrounded her. The water parted. Eshe watched as the crystal columns and a large marble platform rose up from the waves. Sitting royally on the marble recliner was Tolth. Two pale spotted jaguars stood guard over their master.

Eshe didn't move a muscle.

"Come to me, my dear," Tolth's voice wrapped around her and soothed her fears.

Eshe walked cautiously across the mystifying bridge to the beautiful man on the other side. Pearly ribbons of mist that made low whistling noises enveloped her body as she walked. He was the tallest man she had ever seen. His eyes were violet and he had flowing long blond hair. His cloak was blue and partially hid a white sarong.

"Are you here to take me to Heaven?" she asked.

"No, Eshe. I have other plans for you."

Her eyes dropped from his to the pavement. "May I ask your name, my lord?"

"You may, indeed. I am Tolth, Elder of Seras."

"What do you want of me? I am only the daughter of a poor merchant."

He lifted her head by her chin. "You, my child, will be much more than that. You will birth a child and he will be my sword bearer. Through your blood and heritage, my task will be fulfilled and my sins banished."

"My grace, I have never been with a man."

"No, Eshe, I am asking you to carry my child."

"Whoa, whoa, whoa," Julie interrupted.

186

"Is there a problem?" Redderick asked.

"Is this like the virgin story, really?" she asked with a smirk.

"No, not exactly. I believe he may have borrowed the idea," Redderick answered.

"Stolen is more like it."

"Tolth does not have the power to perform virgin births." The immortal nodded courteously. "May I continue?"

"Sure."

As he did with Isa, he waited for Eshe to grant him permission to become the vessel for his seed, and become the sword bearer.

Eshe nodded with her approval.

Tolth slipped his hands under the straps of her gown and let them fall to the ground. She stood before him, nude and unashamed.

Eshe reached out and touched his chest. She moved her hand along the smooth, muscular flesh.

Her hand paused for a mere second as she touched the medallion around his neck.

His fingers tingled down the length of her arms and then he brought her closer to him in one passionate motion. Kissing her, he picked her up, carried her to the cushioned recliner, and made love to her.

"Okay, we can stop right there," Julie interrupted again.

"Very well."

Eshe awoke in her parents' home. They told her how she had been fished out of the well after a tremor had knocked her into the water and she nearly died. Eshe tried to explain what had happened, but no one would believe her.

When her pregnancy began to show, her parents were disgraced, so they expelled her from their home. She became the servant of a Roman commander named Pharaon. He took pity on the girl and gave her a room to live and the help she needed when she went into labor. In return, Eshe fulfilled the duties of a house servant until her dying days.

Eshe gave birth to a baby boy. She named him Kontar. He was to be her only child.

The boy grew up big and strong. He soon became the best wrestler in the region. Pharaon convinced Eshe to let him pull a few strings so Kontar could join the Roman army. Eventually, she agreed. Pharaon renamed him Arian, which meant "the golden life" in Roman to disguise his Hebrew upbringing so the boy could join the legion.

Kontar, now called Arian, traveled across Europe in campaigns for the Empire. In 400 A.D., he was attached to a company moving into Great Britain. There, Arian fell in love with an Anglo-Saxon girl, the daughter of a sheepherder. The two of them escaped in the dark of night into the high hills of the north. Eshe never saw her son again.

The young couple had a single son, Connor. Arian took back his Hebrew name, Kontar, but kept part of his Roman name as his surname Ayr.

Twenty-three years later, Connor and his new bride gave birth to a son, Malcolm. This was the way it stayed for the Ayr family: a single birth of a boy throughout the generations.

Time passed. Wars and rulers came and went. Son after son, the Scottish Ayr clan grew. In the mid-seventeen hundreds, Adrian Ayr, now spelled Ayre, gave birth to a son, Duncan. When war broke out in America in the later part of the century, young Duncan joined a regiment of Royal Highlanders to fight the rebellious colonists.

"My mother just told me about him!" Julie shrieked. "Oh, my gosh! So all of this stuff is true?"

"Of course it is."

"I'm sorry. I just thought…" Julie started to explain.

"No need. I am glad you are starting to understand."

"You are?"

"Of course. That is my job. It will help you, my dear. It will help you understand and make the best choice."

"I do understand. I do. Now, please continue."

"As you wish."

During a skirmish with the Americans, Duncan was wounded. He took shelter in the barn of a small farmhouse in New York. Separated from his unit, Duncan accepted the aide of the farmer's daughter named Arielle. She reluctantly nursed him back to health while fighting her growing feelings for the strapping young man with a funny accent.

Arielle hid Duncan from capture, and the two fell passionately in love. After the War of Independence was over, they were married and had a son, Ian. Duncan changed the spelling of his last name to Ayers in an effort to hide his former allegiance to Great Britain.

Ian's son, Blane, became a successful businessperson. His son, Ewan, fought for the North in the American Civil War. And his son, Steven, moved the family to Ohio. Steven was the great-great-great-great-grandfather to Phillip Ayers.

Phillip Ayers married his high school sweetheart after graduating from college--the first in his family to do so. He and his wife had a son, Patrick. But the small family's happiness was short-lived.

On what seemed to be a typical sunny day in the city for Phillip turned into a chance meeting with Michelle Franklin. The two of them were unnaturally drawn to each other. Eventually, Phillip could not contain his feeling for the lovely woman with brown hair and almond eyes.

His wife, feeling the results of neglect, soon packed up her things and left her husband and son to pursue other possibilities that would give her the attention that she needed.

Phillip Ayers proposed to and married Michelle Franklin. Shortly afterward, Michelle gave birth to a miracle--the first girl born in the Ayers' family history as far back as anyone could remember.

Julie sat in silence.

Chapter Twenty-two

"Julie, what's wrong?" Marcus asked when he saw her face as she returned from her visit with the immortal. He was with Freya, Pertheus, and Griffus.

"Nothing. Can...we...go...now?" she answered in slow, short bursts. The others looked at her in concern.

"Yes, of course." Marcus turned to his fellow council members. "We will resume this later." He then followed her into the cabin and lit the symbol on the floor to open the portal.

After the swirling wind stopped, Julie got up, scurried up the stairs, and closed the basement door. When he caught up with her, she was waiting in his living room.

"What happened?" he asked, as she clutched onto him, burying her face into his chest. When she pulled away, her eyes streamed with tears. "What did he say to you?" Marcus's anger rose to its boiling point.

"Nothing. He just told me something I don't like to think about."

"What?"

She led him to the couch by the hand and sat down. "Have you ever thought about it?"

He sat beside her and gave an affectionate squeeze to her shoulder. "About what?"

Her face showed signs that she fumbled for the words to say. She blew out a deep breath. "Okay, you know how I'm supposed to be this Heart thing, right?" She looked at him and waited for acknowledgment. Once he gave it she continued. "And that I am the first female born on my dad's side of the family since…since God knows when, apparently. Well, in the back of my mind I always thought it was wrong, that it was a mistake and that everything would go back to normal."

"I'm with you so far," he said, trying his best to give comfort.

"Well, two things happened today." She looked him in the eye. "One, he told me something just like my mom told me at dinner the night you were there."

"What?"

"Promise me that you didn't tell him anything?" she asked.

"Julie, I promise. I don't talk to him at all."

"He told me about Duncan Ayre, the guy who was my great-great-grandfather. If he knows that story, then everything else is true."

"I tried to tell you…" Marcus stopped, now wasn't the time. "What else did he say?"

"He reminded me that my dad was married before I was born."

"I didn't know that."

"I am the first born daughter of my mom, and the first born daughter in the Ayer's family, but dad was married once before and had Patrick, then he divorced her to marry my mom."

"I'm sorry. I didn't--"

"Know, I know. This, this…curse has ruined the lives of my family for thousands of years. It caused my dad to get divorced."

Marcus patted her on the knee. "I don't understand why this is upsetting you."

"Because what if my dad was totally happy with his first wife? They were high school sweethearts for crying out loud. He loved her, but this curse made him drop everything and leave his wife to marry my mom just so that I could be born."

"Julie, it's not your fault."

"I know it's not my fault. It's Tolth's fault!" she yelled. "I hate him!"

"Julie."

Julie hopped up. "Don't 'Julie' me. I do," she fumed. "Even before I was born he was ruining my life. Hell, he ruined my entire family's life. I don't get it."

"Then you know what you have to do," Marcus said. He remained seated, trying to preserve peace.

She frowned. "Not now. I have to go." Julie headed for the door.

"I understand," he said.

"No, stop. I don't want you to be understanding right now."

"What do you want me to be?" Marcus stood.

Julie growled and shook her head.

~ * ~

Julie waited a week before confronting Redderick Bobo once again. "I have some questions for you," she said, taking him by surprise as he was walking through his garden.

"I am sure you do. I have been waiting." He continued to rummage through the plants as he talked.

"Cool. Then can we get started?" Julie asked.

"I thought we already had. What questions do you have?"

She looked at him and shrugged. "Fine, we can do this right here."

"Splendid."

"Why did Tolth do what he did? Why did he go to those poor girls and ruin their lives?"

"That's what you heard? He believed he was saving their lives. Look at Isa. What would have happened to her if Lord Tolth had not intervened?"

"I, uh," she stuttered.

"Isla would have died at the hands of the High Priest. And, Eshe?" he asked.

"She would've…"

"She would've died at the bottom of the well. Lord Tolth rescued both of them and turned them into treasures to behold in the eyes of Seras."

"What happened to him?" she asked him. "What happened to Tolth after he went to Earth?" Her tone was serious, surprising even herself. "That wasn't the end of his plan."

"You are correct, my dear. When he came back to Seras, he waited for Bhjuda Heilshorn to return from his quest to retrieve the Stones of Speculus, which then became the Bones of Azahleah."

"My loyal servants," Tolth began, "You have done great works here and I expect you to do many more great things. Bhjuda, I need you to gather an army. Go in search of refugees and those who are in need. Free them, train them, and prepare them for what is to come. Eryx will return, and when she does, she will be more powerful than before. Your army will need to know that. They need to be ready. Once you gather your army, the Solia Custor will be revealed and he will prepare to retrieve my gift." Tolth placed his hand on Heilshorn's heart. "Your time on Seras is complete."

Bhjuda masked his disappointment and nodded stoically.

"He did his job very well, and I am sure that you have been told about his bravery. When Marcus left to find you, he vanished," Redderick finished.

"Did he have a choice?" Julie asked.

"Neither of us knows," he answered.

She studied him for a moment. "What about you?" she asked.

He reared his head back and laughed. "Oh, my child, do you think I am going to tell you what my future holds? I may not even know."

"Don't give me that." She twisted her mouth to the side.

"Heilshorn had his orders. Ostram was to stay out of harm until he…" the immortal paused as if to think of something.

"Yes-s-s-s," Julie said, snapping Redderick out of his stupor.

"Oh, yes, yes, until he met the Solia Custor. Once he did that, he, too, disappeared from Seras." He got up from his seat and moved to a table to pour himself a drink.

"So Heilshorn and Ostram are gone. What happened to Tolth?" Julie asked. She noticed his behavior but decided to ask Marcus more about that later.

"After starting his plan and revealing it to Ostram, Bhjuda, and myself, he had one more thing left to do." Redderick Bobo took a drink. "Would you like some water?" he asked.

"No, I'm good."

Lord Tolth went to the tribe of his creation, the Corven. The Corven tribe continued to worship Tolth under the persecution of the Skorei. He appeared to them in his temple. The ground trembled and the fires lit throughout the cavernous room flickered before roaring and extinguishing. The women fell to their knees and shielded their faces.

Tolth stood before them. The smoke of his flume cleared. He clapped once and the flames reappeared. "Please rise," he said.

When the head priestess was helped to her feet, Tolth touched her on the shoulder. Freshness entered her aged face. She nodded as if to understand unspoken communication between them.

The priestess went by and touched each of the other ten women in the temple. They, in turn, moved in unison. Four approached him as others moved to a separate room. He held out his arms and they guided him to a spacious room.

Two women loosened an aqueduct that flowed with a milky white liquid. Two other priestesses poured almond and vanilla extract mixed with honey into the pool as others were stirring the royal concoction with long, chiseled poles.

With his arms still outstretched, the women removed his robe and led him into the sweet smelling liquid. They bathed him slowly in a ceremonious fashion. Afterward, he motioned them to the altar. They followed without a word. Lord Tolth sat down on the altar. A brilliant sword appeared by his side. He touched the head priestess gently on the temple. "I have a favor to ask of you."

She looked at the sword and backed away. "No, my lord. I cannot do such a thing."

He smiled and nodded at her. "I have faith that you can and will."

"But why?"

"This is my final act. I must make what has become of Seras right and prepare a way to defeat what is to come."

She took the sword and held it in her hands. Her eyes betrayed the fact she did not control her actions.

A clay jar appeared. "I give you the knowledge to do what you must when the opportunity presents itself," he told her. He could see his words did not make sense to her, but he had to proceed. "Lift up the sword." His words echoed in her head, and she obeyed. "The essence of my being will retreat to this jar. Keep it until evil makes itself known to you."

"My lord." Tears welled in her eyes.

"It is time."

She raised the sword over her head and plunged it toward Tolth's abdomen. As the tip pierced his skin, he vanished. A glowing substance replaced his body and gathered and floated toward the jar. Once the particles were inside, a priestess closed a lid on the clay container.

Tolth was gone and the priestesses woke from their mental haze. The only remnants were the sword, still in the hands of the head priestess, and the clay jar.

The women stared at each other for a moment before returning to their daily routines. And they waited. They waited for over one thousand years.

Chapter Twenty-three

"Happy birthday to you, happy birthday to you!" Julie's mom and dad opened her door and walked in. Julie raised her head off the pillow to see her mom carrying a small cake and her dad unsuccessfully hiding something behind his back.

"What are you two doing?" she asked, moving to sit up and rubbing the sleep out of her eyes.

"Celebrating our favorite daughter's birthday," her father joked.

Julie twisted her face. "I don't even have to say it."

"Oh, honey, we love you so much," her mother shrieked as she sat on the bed beside her and gave her a hug.

"Okay, what are you hiding?"

"What are you talking about?" he asked with a sly smile and wink.

"We can do better than that," her mother said. With a look at Phillip they said in unison, "Look outside!"

Julie reared back at their excitement, hopped up on all fours and peered out of her bedroom window. "Oh, my gosh!" she shrieked. Sitting in the driveway was a dark purple two-door car. She began hopping up and down, bouncing on the bed, and clapping her hands rapidly like hummingbird wings. "Are you kidding me?"

"Nope." Philip held out his hand and two shiny silver keys dangled from his fingers. "You've been driving your mom's minivan long enough."

"Yep. I'm ready to get my car back," Michelle said, smiling and giving Julie another hug.

"Can I go look at it?"

"Of course, of course!" they answered.

Julie hustled down the stairs and out the door without her socks or shoes, her mom and dad fast behind her. The new-to-her car was small and compact, just perfect for Julie. "Oh, my gosh, I love it!" She hopped in the front seat. "How in the world?"

Her mother pointed a thumb at her father. "He found it and spent the past month fixing it and cleaning it up."

Julie popped out of the seat and gave her dad a big hug. "I love it! Thank you both!" She then gave her mom a hug before climbing back into the driver's seat and starting it up. Michelle helped herself to the passenger seat. Julie backed the car enough to point it the right direction and zoomed away.

That night, Julie's family and friends gathered at her house to celebrate her big occasion. "I can't believe you all are here," Julie said in true surprise. The car her parents bought her would have sufficed. *Sufficed? Now there's a big word, Jules*, she thought. *I wonder if they're trying to overcompensate for last year.* She paused to hug a guest at the party and thank them for coming. *Overcompensate. Wow, I'm breaking out the big guns tonight.*

Claire and Jimmy met her in the kitchen. "Happy birthday, Jules." Claire hugged her.

Jimmy gave her the awkward side hug. "Happy birthday."

"Thank you." Julie clapped semi-nervously. "I loved the message you sent me," she told Claire. It was a long audio of Claire singing a twangy country version of "Happy Birthday."

A knock on the door interrupted their conversation and sent Julie's mother to welcome the new guest. Julie peeked around the corner to see who would walk in.

It was Mr. Campbell. Julie took a slow, deliberate walk toward him. She didn't want to come off as too excited, but inside, her night felt complete. Julie waited for her mother to greet him and then gave him the same side-by-side hug Jimmy just gave her. "Hey."

"Hi," he said as Michelle ushered him into the entryway.

"I'm glad you could make it."

"I wouldn't miss it," he answered, making his way to the kitchen. Her mother offered him a drink and handed him a red plastic cup. Mr. Campbell accepted it, took a sip, and turned his attention back to her.

Claire and Jimmy joined them. "Hi, Mr. C.," they both took turns saying. Jimmy stuck out his hand and Mr. Campbell shook it.

"Did you see her new car?" Claire asked, giving their teacher a side hug.

"No?" He looked at Julie with a proud smile.

"New-to-me car," Julie corrected with a shrug.

"You should see it," Claire added.

"I'm sorry. There were too many cars outside to--"

"Don't sweat, Mr. C. I'm sure you'll see it some time," Julie said.

"So, what did you name it?" he asked, taking another drink from his cup.

Julie cocked her head to the side and gave him an unsure look. "How did you know?"

Jimmy excused himself to get another drink and Claire followed.

"How did I know? You told me. Remember last year, you gave me a hard time about not having a name for my car?"

"Oh, yeah." She smiled. "I can't believe you remembered that," she said with a laugh.

"Of course I did."

"Jelly Bean," she said, taking a drink of punch.

"Excuse me?"

"You heard me. I named my car Jelly Bean." She brushed a strand of hair behind her ear.

"Really?" he asked in a perplexed tone.

"Yep!"

"What happened to using a girl's name?"

Julie hopped up on the counter. Sitting there she could look at him eye-to-eye. "Wait until you see it, and then you'll see why I named it Jelly Bean."

The sound of her mother clearing her throat behind her caused Julie to hop back off of the counter. "Um, young lady," Michelle admonished her.

"Sorry." Julie shrunk.

"Let's not get carried away," her mother said, before pulling a metal pan out of the oven and arranging the piping hot snacks on a glass plate.

"Okay, let me introduce you to some of my family," Julie said. She moved out of the kitchen to the living room where guests were sitting comfortably on the couch, loveseat and two matching chairs. Two couples were sharing the couch. "This is my Aunt Patty and Uncle Walt, and Aunt Katie and Uncle Roy," she said. "This is Mr. Campbell, my history teacher."

"Marcus," she corrected as the men leaned up to shake Mr. Campbell's hand. Their wives stayed seated as Mr. C. reached down to them.

"They're not really related," Julie explained to Mr. Campbell. "That's just what I've always called them."

"Nice to meet you," her Aunt Katie said. "We've heard so much about you. It's nice to finally put a face to the name." Aunt Katie was a tall, slender brunette with blue eyes.

Her Aunt Patty was the complete opposite: short, plump, blonde with green eyes. "I am so happy we finally get to meet you," Aunt Patty flirted.

"Okay," Julie said. "I think I'll leave on that note."

"You can go." Aunt Patty shooed her away with a wave of her hand. "Just leave him here with me."

Julie saw Mr. C's face turn scarlet.

"Here, you probably need a new one of these." Her father approached carrying two glasses of wine. "Especially if you're talking to these four." He handed one of the glasses to Marcus.

"Thank you," he said, taking the glass and a sip.

With that, Julie left to mingle with her friends until later that night when her parents brought out a birthday cake for her and led everyone in a round of "Happy Birthday."

This day is one thousand times better than last year's birthday, she thought as she blew out the seventeen candles. "Thank you, everyone!" Then a thought hit her as she looked at all of their cheerful faces, laughing, clapping, and having a great time. *There is something I have to do.*

Chapter Twenty-four

The sound of the basement door groaned slowly as Mr. Campbell opened it up and stepped into his living room. His steps were cautious and quiet. The pain of the night was still hauntingly fresh in her mind. "Why did I go?" she asked, covering her face and sitting on his couch.

"Are you sorry you did?" her teacher's voice whispered behind her. She didn't want to turn around and let him see the fat tears running down her cheeks.

"What do you think?" she asked in a hushed voice, trying to fight back the lump in her throat. "There was nothing there but dead ground." Her visit to Callista's burial site was nothing like she expected.

The misty morning started under a bad omen. When Julie pulled up in her purple car, the rain was coming down in full force. The blacktop parking lot shimmered in the pouring rain. She hustled to Mr. Campbell's door and pounded on it rapidly. "Come on, come on."

He opened the door and ushered her in. "What are you doing? I thought you would take today off."

"No, there is something I need to do." She shook with a chill.

"Do you want a towel?" He started to head upstairs.

"No, I'm good. Besides," she raised her hands to chest height, palms up, and shrugged, "we're going to be dry as soon as we pass through the portal."

"Well, yeah, but your clothes will be wet when we return."

"I don't care," she snapped. "I'll deal with that when we get back." Julie started for the basement.

"Okay. Mind telling me what's going on?" He pressed the door closed.

She sighed. "Please," Julie begged, "I want to see Callista." She was determined.

"Do you think that's a good idea?" Mr. Campbell asked but then switched topics. "Can I get you something to eat or drink?" He started for the small kitchen area.

"Yes, I think it's a good idea. That's why I'm here." Julie reached out to stop him. "And, no thanks. I'm good. I had a bowl of cake and cereal before I came."

"Cake and cereal?" He looked worried about her decision, as well as disgusted with her breakfast of choice.

"The breakfast choice of all saviors of Seras," she joked as she opened the basement door. "Can we go now?"

"Okay. I will take you." He sighed and then followed her down the stairs to the portal.

The mood of Seras's fog-gray sunless sky matched Julie's. "There isn't anything marking the graves," Julie whispered as she navigated through the lush countryside where Callista was buried. The field, fertilized by fire and death, expanded across what Marcus reminded her was the seldom visited western flank of Allon. To her, the ground took on the life of its fallen champions.

The blue-gray sky gave little light to their footsteps as the student and her teacher wandered through the maze-like patches to find the resting place of her beloved friend. "Couldn't you have built her a memorial or something?"

"We don't do things like that here," Marcus answered. He was wearing a full-length brown cloak over his deer hide pants and white cotton shirt. His attire differed from her dyed green cloak and leathered pants and top, but she smiled at thinking in some way they matched each other, and she matched the rich terrain.

"Well, maybe you should start."

"Julie," he turned to look at her. His eyes revealed sadness and worry. Suddenly, Marcus stopped. "This is the place," he said through the mist.

Julie swallowed hard. The lump in her throat tightened. Her eyes began to burn with strained tears. Without thinking, Julie's knees slammed against the ground in front of the spot Marcus had stopped. "Callista," she cried softly. Her body shook as Marcus placed his hand on her shoulder. "Hi. I know you're not here, but I had to say goodbye." A pool of tears drenched her cloak. "I'm sorry it took me so long to visit. You'll be happy to know that Mr. C….Marcus has been working my butt off." Her voice broke. "I'm so sorry, Callista. I miss you so much."

Marcus clutched her shoulder tighter. "Julie..." his voice trailed off. She felt his grip release and his footsteps fade.

"I'm not sure where you are. I guess in Speculus, wherever that is. I hope you forgive me. You wanted me to be something I'm not. You trusted me." Tears streamed harder down her cheeks. "You trusted me, and I let you down...I let you die." Julie's hands snapped up to her face, shielding her eyes, trying to hide the pain. "I miss you!" she screamed. "I miss everything about you. I wish there was a way I could make it up to you. I wish I could be the person you thought I was, and save you." Her body trembled uncontrollably. Julie heard the rustle of Marcus's feet move through the grass.

"Jules, we should go," he said softly behind her.

"Okay," Julie said, she stood and made one final comment as she wiped her hand across her nose. "I promise I will take care of him. You know he's helpless without you."

"Julie," his voice pleaded, "are you okay?" He stood firm as she tried to walk away.

"You're kidding, right?"

Now, sitting there in Marcus's living room, her teacher repeated that question. "Julie, are you okay?"

Her response was exactly the same. "You're kidding, right?" She took the mug of hot chocolate he handed her. Julie held it in both hands, pursed her lips, and blew the steam away from her face.

Marcus sat down next to her. "You wanna talk about it?"

She shrugged. "I doubt it would help."

"You can try."

"She had all of this faith in me. That faith led to her death. You have faith in me. How do you think that makes me feel?"

"I--"

"No, it's my turn." She looked at him, prepared for an argument that didn't come. "I'm worried. I'm scared, Marcus," she paused, wondering where that came from. "Seras is poison to me. It holds me against my will. It strangles me and leaves scars all over my heart. I can't scream, I can't talk to anybody, I can't escape. I'm locked in this silent prison of darkness, no, worse than that. I can't even close my eyes because I still see visions of that day or I see you or Redderick Bobo. I'm stuck in this private, personal hell."

"What can I say to help you?" Marcus placed his hand on the upper part of her back.

"Nothing," she said. "Just get me through this so I can have a normal life someday."

"I'll try my best."

"Thank you."

Chapter Twenty-five

"Jules, come on down!" her father called from downstairs. It had been four weeks since Julie's visit to Callista's grave. Since then, she had placed a marker on the spot and picked wildflowers to place at her friend's final resting spot.

Julie hopped out of bed and threw her hair in a ponytail. She bounded down the stairs to the wonderful aroma of her dad's pancakes. "Yum!" She clapped in excitement. "Did you make any blueberry ones?"

"Of course, I did," he answered. "I know what my little girl likes." He flipped the frying pan and two pancakes somersaulted in the air before landing safely back in the pan.

"When are we leaving for the parade?" she asked, sitting down at the table to wait for her dad to deliver the goods.

"It starts at ten, so we have plenty of time." Phillip scooped up three blueberry pancakes with his spatula and put them on her plate.

"Cool." Julie began happily eating her breakfast.

The village of Sunset was busier than normal to celebrate Independence Day. The new organizer took note of the limited success of the first-ever Chocolate Festival and added a large stage with different musical guests from morning until night. The only break would be the hour-long parade.

Julie stayed just ahead of her parents as they walked from one of the parking spots at Cedar Creek High School to the center of town.

"What do you have planned for the day?" Michelle asked as she and Phillip strolled hand-in-hand down the sidewalk to the square. Her father had the straps of two lawn chairs in his other hand.

Julie turned to face her parents, and as she walked backward, she shrugged. "Oh, you know, find Claire and Jimmy, eat some fair fries, drink a few lemon shakes, watch the parade. Normal stuff."

"Sounds like you have it all planned out," her father said, swinging his wife's hand back and forth with exaggerated enthusiasm. "Well, you can go get started if you want."

"Nah, I'm good. They know where to find me." She joined her parents, snuggling between them as she took their hands and skipped slowly to keep pace. Her mom and dad began skipping with her toward the square.

Julie sat in one of the umbrella chairs next to her mother and watched Sunset's annual parade. Her mood was so much better than it was this time last year. Claire and Jimmy joined the family about the time the horse riders made their appearance.

"Hey," Claire said walking up to Julie, holding tight to Jimmy's hand. In his other hand, he held a box of popcorn.

"Hey." Julie sprung up and hugged both of her friends. "Where have you two been?"

"We were by the fountain. I thought you were going to meet us," Claire said, snagging a handful of Jimmy's popcorn.

"I thought we were going to meet here." Julie shrugged. "No worries. You're here now." She turned to her parents. "Is it okay?"

Claire hugged Julie's parents. Jimmy shook her father's hand.

"Of course it is," her father answered. He took Julie's seat and waved goodbye.

The three walked away. "What do you wanna do first?" Claire asked.

"Let's go see who's at the teacher's dunk tank," Julie said, bobbing her head back and forth. "But first, I need some fries." She giggled.

Julie and her friends followed the pavement through the square to one corner of the brick-lined street. Just like every year since she was a little girl, the village had a carnival atmosphere. The teachers of Cedar Creek did their part by volunteering to raise money with their dunk tank. "Same deal as last year?" Julie asked Jimmy.

"Want me to throw left-handed, again?" he answered. Jimmy strutted between Julie and Claire. Claire gave him a playful shove.

"No." Julie crinkled her nose. "I'm going to beat you fair and square this year." She broke into a slow jog and hopped in the line for fries.

"Come on, hot shot." Claire pulled Jimmy by the arm. "Let's go get in line for a lemon shake."

"How is this the same deal as last year?" Jimmy asked, hopping on one foot to keep his balance as Claire tugged on him.

"Psh, like I'm going to stop at one fry," Julie laughed.

After the trio got their shake and fries, they made their way to the dunk tank.

"Oh man, we missed Langston," Jimmy said as they got closer and watched the history teacher and track coach climb down from the tank.

"Dang!" Claire plopped her hand across her forehead. "I would've loved to pay him back for all the four hundreds he made me do during track."

Mr. Campbell walked out of the teachers' changing tent. He was wearing blue and black swimming trunks and a green and yellow Cedar Creek shirt.

"Ooo, hoho, this is going to be fun," Julie said, rubbing her hands together as she plotted sending him into the Plexiglas water tank.

"You're going down!" Claire yelled as the English teacher climbed the ladder and took his place on the tiny seat.

Mr. Campbell turned his head in their direction and then shook it "no."

"Oh, yeah," Julie said as she gave the teacher collecting donations a five dollar bill. The teacher reached to give her back change. ""No, no, keep it. I'm going to get my money's worth."

"Go first," Jimmy said as he paid for three balls.

"Nope. I went first last year."

"Don't worry about them, Marcus," the voice of Mr. Langston rang out as he exited the tent dry and dressed in khaki shorts and a Hawaiian shirt.

"I'm not; I've seen her throw," Mr. Campbell said.

"She throws like a girl," Langston joked.

"Worse, like a cheerleader," Mr. Campbell said.

"Hey, now it's on." Julie crunched her face in determination.

Claire gave her coach a hug. "What's up with the Hawaiian look?"

"This is my Magnum P.I. look," Langston answered, stroking his mustache.

"I don't know who that is." Claire shrugged with an apologetic smile.

"Kids now days." Mr. Langston shook his head, put his arm around Claire, and gave her a friendly side-hug.

Julie's first throw knocked Mr. Campbell into the tank. She then moved over and swept her hand across her chest to allow Jimmy to line up for his throw.

"Lucky shot!" Mr. Langston called out.

Mr. Campbell reemerged, sputtering water out of his mouth and adjusting his goggles. He got reset and Jimmy took aim. Jimmy's first throw missed its target, but his second and third ones sent Mr. Campbell into the water.

"I think I won," Julie said with an air of confidence. She took her position at the line. "Oh, Mr. C. I still have fourteen balls."

Mr. Campbell gave her an exasperated look, and the surrounding teachers, students, and onlookers laughed. Julie dunked him with every single throw.

"That felt good," Julie joked afterward as she and her friends strolled around the square, shopped at the flea market, ate more fries, and drank more lemon shakes.

"I can't believe you dunked him fifteen times, plus Jimmy put him in twice," Claire said. "I felt sorry for him."

Julie smirked. "I didn't. He enjoys torturing me. I'm glad I could pay him back."

"How does he torture you?" Jimmy asked.

"Huh?" Julie stopped and stuttered. "I mean his homework assignments and tests."

"No doubt," Claire said. "But seventeen straight times between the two of you?"

Julie laughed. "Yep!" She took a long drink of her shake.

Later that evening, Julie found her parents sitting in their spot on the bleachers with a group of friends and Mr. Campbell. "Hi," she said to Mr. Campbell. What she really wanted to say was, *What are you doing here?*

"Hi," he answered as she walked past him to kiss her parents and hug many of the people sitting near them.

"Julie, honey, let me look at you," her parents' friend, Susan, said. "You get prettier and prettier every year."

"Thank you, Aunt Susan," Julie said before sitting next to Mr. Campbell.

He cocked his head in confusion.

"Not really my aunt. I've known her and Uncle Bill since forever, though," Julie explained. She then whispered, "That's something we do here on Earth, call our parents' lifelong friends aunt and uncle."

"Everywhere on Earth?" he asked in a hushed tone.

She shrugged. "On all the parts I know." Then she gave him an evil grin. "It looks like you recovered."

"Recovered from what?"

"From me nearly drowning you." Her voice raised in laughter.

"I heard you nearly drowned Mr. Campbell," her mother said.

"See!" Julie said. "You even told my mother. Wait, you told my mom on me?"

"It wasn't like that."

"So you agree that I nearly drowned you." She gave him her cutest look.

"Nah, not even close," Mr. Campbell said with a quick shoulder nudge.

"Liar." Julie smiled. *This Fourth of July was a thousand times better than last year.*

Chapter Twenty-six

Marcus watched as Julie took aim with her bow. They decided to ease up on the fencing practice and work on other skills that are necessary in combat. She let loose an arrow and it struck the round barrel lid they hung up on a tree. The arrow landed just on the edge.

"Okay, not a kill shot, but you're getting closer," Marcus told her. He looked at the misfires lying scattered on the ground, nearby trees, and up and down the tree holding the target.

"Ugh! I'm never going to get the hang of this," Julie fumed. She shook her arm. "My forearm is killing me."

"It gets easier."

"And I hate that you call them kill shots," she grumbled. "I don't ever want to kill somebody."

"I know. I'm sorry."

A bell sounded from the fortress wall. Both straightened up in surprise. "What's that mean?" Julie asked.

"Grab our stuff and get to the cabin," Marcus commanded as he ran toward his horse. He mounted quickly and took off toward the gate. He turned to see Julie start to grab the bags of food and water then toss them down. She hopped on her horse and started galloping after him.

"The eastern wall," a soldier yelled down to Marcus from his post on the rampart.

As he led his steed through the streets, he could hear Julie close behind.

A crowd had gathered on the interior of the wall as the small passage door was closed by a soldier, and the large eastern gate was opened. It appeared that everyone had already beaten him and Julie to the sight.

Dozens of exhausted looking women, children, and old men entered from the opened gate. Marcus dismounted. Julie sprang up to him. He gave her a concerned look.

"I know, I shouldn't be here," she said in a near whisper.

"No, you shouldn't. This could have been dangerous."

A familiar woman stood in the presence of those surrounding her.

Marcus noticed an emblem of Hawkmir, an opened wing bird of prey, on the chest plate of one of the old men entering Allon. Marcus averted his face from those who passed by him. He moved closer to the center of the circle where Freya, Argos, and Julius were to avoid being recognized.

"Jayna, what is going on?" Marcus asked. He stayed low enough to avoid being seen, yet upright not to make Julie question what he was doing.

"I had to, Marcus."

Argos spoke up to explain. "Jayna has been spying in Cauleta; since the Battle of Yellow Fields Tanda has been working together to keep us informed on what activities Pallanex or William have been up to." Argos ran a hand along his narrow face and through his brown hair with touches of gray. "Jayna has been there helping her. We would hate to be caught off guard again," he finished.

"Why are all of these people here?" Freya asked. Her tone was impatient.

Jayna apologized again, her voice strained from the long journey. She took a long drink given to her by Seren who had joined the group. "William marched on the Hawkmir. He killed every man in the fort."

"I didn't know there was a fort," Marcus started to say before stopping to think about what he was saying and who he was saying it in front of.

"I watched the whole thing. I couldn't help them. I had to save them," Jayna cried.

"So you brought them here?" Freya questioned, barely waiting for Jayna to catch her breath.

Argos stopped Freya's interrogation, looking at the poor souls entering Allon. "This isn't the place. Let's go inside and hear what happened." He turned to his oldest son. "Take them to the market square; get them some food and water."

Julius started to walk away. "What about shelter?"

"Set up tents wherever you can find room. Grab some pillows and blankets from as many quarters available," Argos answered.

"Is that wise?" Freya asked.

"It's the right thing to do," Argos answered. "Go."

Julius turned and moved toward the front of the Hawkmir people to lead them in the right direction.

Argos gave Seren a look suggesting action. "Go help."

Julie watched Marcus wave his hand to a soldier. The man brought a horse to him. He helped the Tarrack woman up on the large beast. "I'll take her to the council cabin."

Marcus mounted his horse, Julie did the same.

Inside the council room, Marcus, Julie, Freya, and Argos were joined by Pertheus and Griffus to hear Jayna tell about William's battle against the Hawkmir people. "I watched from the side of a mountain away from harm. I knew there was nothing I could do once William crossed the river. I decided the only thing I could do was to save as many of the people I could still inside the fort. I flew down and convinced the women and children to exit out of the rear of the ruins. The men who stayed gave their lives to hold off William and his army as long as they could until I could get them deep into the woods."

"William didn't pursue you?" Freya asked.

"No, I never heard his men give chase. Once we left I followed the paths through the Evandell Forest until we enter the Lobello Mountains," Jayna explained. "It was a slow journey."

"You did well," Argos said, patting her on the back.

Marcus looked at Julie. She was studying everyone's faces. Their dire expressions were not giving her confidence. "Thank you, Jayna. You need to get some rest."

The Tarrack woman got up to leave the room. "I should have done more. I should have helped the men fight William," Jayna said as tears welled up in her eyes.

"No, then neither you nor the people you saved would be here," Marcus told her. "You did the right thing."

"Thank you," she said.

Argos got up and escorted her out the door.

Pertheus moved to follow Jayna. "I'll go with her then I will check on the new arrivals."

"Now what do we do?" Griffus asked.

"We need move on Cauleta. William and Pallanex are comfortable, and I don't like it," Freya said.

"We aren't ready," Marcus argued, shaking his head.

"When will we be ready?" Freya shot back. "I have given you over a year. We have sat doing nothing, waiting for you to be ready. We have strengthened our walls. We've doubled our spies in Cauleta..."

"I know you have. I've told you how impressed I am with what you have done. We just can't do it right now."

"It's been a year, Marcus!" Freya raised her voice, gazing deep into his eyes. "When will you be ready?"

"I am afraid I agree with Marcus," the voice of Redderick Bobo interrupted the argument between the two siblings. The remaining council stopped and stared at the immortal. "Julie, my dear, would you like to join me."

Julie, who had been silent through the scene, looked at Marcus for advice. Marcus nodded his approval. Julie got up and left with Redderick Bobo without saying a word.

"Don't ever challenge me in front of her again, Freya," Marcus said in a low growl.

"When are you going to let her see what she can do, Marcus?" Freya asked.

"Now, now, you two need to stop this," Griffus said, holding up his walking stick over the table to separate them.

"I will let her, when she is ready, and not just because you want to test her," he answered.

~*~

"Are they going to be okay," Julie asked Redderick as they left the council cabin.

"Ah, yes, just sibling fights," he answered. "I am glad you are back, I have been growing old waiting for you," Redderick said as she pulled the door flap back and motioned for her to enter.

"Ha, that's a good one," she said.

"A good what?" The immortal poured himself a drink and took a leisurely sip.

"Nothing, I'm really glad to see you too," Julie said with an air of sarcasm. "I sure have missed our little chats together." His harem stared at her with disdain.

"Yes, have a seat." Redderick sat down and brushed his vest off of his belly.

Julie closed her eyes to keep the grotesque image out of her mind, but it was too late. "So, what's today's story?"

"Ah, I hope you find this one very educational," he started in a condescending tone.

I probably deserved that, she thought.

Redderick Bobo began his story.

Two brothers, Canis and Theon, were disciples of Eryx and warlords of Seras. Canis was tall and handsomely chiseled. He had dark, shoulder-length hair, a groomed goatee, and piercing blue eyes. Theon was built like a human bull--thick-necked and barrel-chested. His hair was blond but thinning. The tribe their father left them was divided into two equal shares. At the request of their dominating mother, Cauleta, they joined their forces to rule evenly. It is not difficult to predict what happened.

Canis was an accomplished warrior. He fought more fluidly than his lumbering brother, though one strike of Theon's mighty ax ended any opponent standing in his way. They lorded over their combined armies and a large portion of Seras for many years. Theon was satisfied with controlling their portion of Seras while Canis wanted more. Theon knew his brother wanted more, he just did not know the lengths his brother would go to to achieve his goals.

Shortly after their mother died, Canis met secretly with Urvasus, the leader of a fierce warrior tribe, the Tarracks. The Tarracks are shape-shifting creatures that can change from human to bear to hawk to cougar. The two plotted to unseat Theon as Canis's equal.

Urvasus moved his tribe into the region outside of Theon and Canis's kingdom. Canis sent spies to report to Theon that the Tarracks were plotting to attack. Finally, Theon, convince by the false information and the constant council of Canis, agreed to wage war on the Tarracks.

Theon and his generals chose their positions to advance the center of the front line and split Canis's army to flank either side of the Tarracks. This plan worked perfectly for Canis.

Under Theon's command, the army advanced to a place that would take them within an hours' ride of the Tarrack encampment. Theon halted the men and to set up a temporary base before nightfall.

"The night before a battle," Theon said as he and Canis moved toward a warm fire, "there is no feeling I crave more."

"Then why not have more nights like these?" Canis asked. Though Theon did not know it, it was a last minute plea to stop his plan.

"No, we have done what our father wanted, and he and Mother would be proud."

"We could do so much more. Think about what we have done and what we could do together."

"Rest, little brother," Theon said, rubbing his hands for additional warmth. "It is a chilly night."

Canis gave up his appeal. "Yes, it is. We should have brought women."

"You are against having women in our company."

"I am against taking them as wives. I am not against having them in our company. Tonight feels like a three-whore night."

Theon laughed heartily. "We have a long day ahead of us tomorrow."

The next morning, when Theon moved against Uravasus, the Tarracks were ready. Wave after wave of hawks from the air and bears and cougars from the ground and trees pounced upon Theon and his men. Canis took the opportunity to move against Theon. The ferocious Canis faced off against his brother. Theon wielded his mighty ax. Canis was armed with a double-edged broadsword.

The two brothers battled with sword and ax and exchanged fierce blows. The forest erupted with their intensity. Canis's army, with the help of the Tarracks, seized control of Theon's men. Theon was not so easily defeated. Theon got close enough to grab Canis by the throat. The air closed off around Canis. Theon growled in his brother's face. The spit sprayed as Theon said, "You traitorous worm. Mother would be so disappointed. I will destroy you."

Theon released his grip and Canis sunk to the ground, his left hand clutched his throat. Theon took aim with a large swing meant to decapitate his younger brother. Canis took his right hand and grabbed Theon's leg, knocking him off balance. The ax buried deep into a tree.

Theon could not wrench it free fast enough as Canis pounded him with a rock-clenched fist. Before Theon could shake off the blows, Canis was standing above him, a sword resting in both hands in front of his face, pausing long enough for Theon to think that his brother had changed his mind.

"Brother," Theon spoke with heartfelt sincerity.

Canis flipped the sword in his hand and plunged it into the thick chest of his older brother. Theon's body jerked and then lay limp. Canis pulled his sword out of Theon's body and raised it over his head. All of his men cheered in celebration. The Tarracks offered emblems of a treaty between themselves and the new warlord. Those loyal to Theon were given a chance to convert or die.

The alliance between Canis and Urvasus lasted the rest of Canis's life.

Canis and his army began seizing power from other warlords. He then moved to conquer other tribes. The Evandell were among the first to fall and were used as slaves. Being in complete control, he ruled with a reign of terror unlike anything Seras had ever seen. That ended when he fell in love with a Corven maiden of medium height with golden brown hair and hazel eyes.

"Wait, like Freya?" Julie asked, breaking into Redderick's story.

"Yes, like Freya," the immortal huffed. "Raewin, the Corven maiden, was Freya's mother."

"So this is about Marcus's family." She cocked her head sideways.

"Canis was Marcus's father and Raewin was his mother," he said.

"What does this have to do with me?" Julie asked, hopping up from the pillowed couch.

"Sit down, sit down, my dear. All will be explained." Redderick Bobo patted the space next to him.

"Okay, but I have questions." She plopped down reluctantly but curious for more information.

"I am sure you do." He nodded with a grin. "May I continue?"

Julie sighed. "Yes."

"Thank you. As I was saying, Canis fell in love with the Corven maiden Raewin. The first time he saw her she was wearing a red top with a single thin strap hanging off of her shoulder. The only problem this caused for Canis was his reputation for not allowing his men to take wives. He made his marriage promise to her in secret. That night his first son was conceived."

"Um, we can skip that whole part, thank you very much," Julie said with a grimace.

"Very well."

Due to Canis's circumstances, he had a change of heart. He declared that his men could begin taking wives and he created a permanent settlement for him and his men. His men were confused, but relieved. The settlement started modestly. It consisted of a central place for Canis, cabins for his men and their future families, and a large arena for training the young men that would be born. He called it Cauleta. He showed off the progress made by the hard work he and his men put into the settlement to Urvasus the Tarrack. The two strolled through the developing encampment.

"Cauleta?" Urvasus asked. He was a big man. It was said that very little changed when he transformed from a man to a bear.

"My mother's name," Canis answered. He held out his arms. "She would be proud."

"Indeed," Urvasus said. "I must admit, I am surprised you decided to finally build a structure such as this." Canis escorted Urvasus into his animal-hide home. "You do have a long way to go," Urvasus joked.

"This is not the end. I plan on turning the lumbered walls into thick fortress ones. I want Cauleta to be a place known throughout the lands." The two sat on logged seats and drank frothing ale from a pitcher.

Once the fortress was complete, Canis invited Raewin into his home. She rejected the proposal. As a Corven maiden, she felt it was her duty to stay close to her tribe's beliefs and worship the Elder Tolth, something she would not be able to do in Cauleta. While Canis was a product of Eryx, he was not an active worshiper of the elderess. He could not allow the worship of Tolth inside his walls and keep the loyalty of his men. Raewin maintained a modest hut deep in the woods. It was a day journey from Cauleta, but she was free to practice the ways of the Corven without drawing the ire of Canis's tribe. Raewin gave birth to Marcus in her hut in the woods.

As per the ritual of his time, Canis took his newborn son and presented him to the midnight sky. "You, Marcus, the first son born to Canis of Cauleta, were formed in the image of your father. You will be forged in the fire of battle. You will not fear man or death. Men will learn to fear your name."

Raewin took care of Marcus until he was able to walk. Then she relinquished her duties of motherhood to Canis. All in an attempt to woo his wife to his home, the city of Cauleta had grown in size and beauty.

Canis made sure Marcus had proper early training and gave him over to the training methods of Kralen. Two years later, Darius was born, and the same routine was followed. Three years after that, Freya was born.

Upon her birth, as was tradition for the Corven, Raewin took Freya to a Corven temple and laid her in a basket placed in the middle of a chiseled symbol of the Elders. With incense, milk, and water said to have been from the bath of Tolth, the temple priestess welcomed the child as a Corven maiden.

Canis agreed to let Raewin raise Freya as a Corven as she did not have the necessary bloodline to be accepted into Canis's tribe. Though in later years, Freya would visit her father for short stints. Raewin continued rejecting Canis's offers, even with the promise of protecting her religion.

Marcus and Darius were trained in combat by the towering hulk Kralen. The two sons grew to be among the most brutal fighters in the school and made their father very proud. In later years, Marcus and Darius graduated from combat training and joined their father in true battles. Both were skilled and moved up the ranks quickly through fierce fighting and clever strategies.

Two things happened that changed the future of Canis, his sons, and his men. First, Canis met another woman. She was a wandering follower of Eryx, displaced by her leaders as being dangerous and unholy. Little did they know that was the type of follower Eryx would have preferred. She was young, beautiful, and flirty. She moved with a slow, seductive saunter. She had blue streaks in her raven hair. She seduced the aging Canis. This was Pallanex.

"Pallanex!" Julie repeated.

"Yes," Redderick answered.

"What does she have to do with this?" Julie asked.

"Give me time, child. Pallanex gave Marcus's father, Canis, bad council."

This council was the second mistake Canis made. Pallanex in her wily ways convinced Canis to attack and destroy all of the Corven tribes. Eventually, Canis and his army made their way to the Corven temple that held the essence of Tolth in the clay pottery. Prior to the head priestess being murdered, she followed the instructions that had been passed down from generation to generation. She made her way inside the temple, releasing the contents of the container. The room was filled with Tolth's glory. The priestess chanted a curse and light stormed through the warriors, knocking them off their feet. With the death of the Corven priestesses, the remains of Tolth, weakened by the centuries of being inside the clay jar, struck the warrior, and made its way to the only two surviving priestesses of Tolth, Raewin and her daughter, Freya. The effects on the warriors were not life threatening but left a permanent result: the warriors were unable to reproduce. This would cripple them in their ability to maintain their army.

Beautiful Pallanex, who had made her home inside the palace walls, had big plans. She stroked the ego of Canis by creating a large courtyard with marble images of Canis, his eldest son, Marcus, Kralen, the respected trainer of many warriors, and the elderess, Eryx. She then seduced a young friend of Marcus's. The impressionable warrior's head was filled with thoughts of grandeur. Pallanex convinced him to lead a raid against Canis's wife, Raewin. Raewin, who was alone after letting Freya visit her father in Cauleta, fought well, but in the end, she succumbed to the young warrior's blade.

With Raewin dead, Pallanex was named queen. Once again, she convinced the young friend of Marcus, who was nearly a son to Canis, to lead those loyal to the newly appointed queen to attack Marcus, Darius, and Freya.

The plan was in motion. Marcus's friend sent a unit of fifty soldiers against the three siblings. At the time, Marcus had celebrated his eighteenth Tempora. Marcus and Darius fought a bloody battle against the traitorous soldiers. Freya cowered behind her brothers. Marcus's friend had a change of heart after watching his friend fight so valiantly. He joined the fray, and alongside Marcus and Darius, the three overcame the guards.

While that was going on in a different area of the palace gardens, Queen Pallanex had Canis in her chamber.

"Canis, can I pour you a drink, my love?" Queen Pallanex asked in a soft purr.

The mighty Canis, whose dark hair and thinning beard that once framed his dignified face was now white as snow, nodded in approval. Queen Pallanex poured two drinks and handed a chalice to him.

"To you, my husband." She bowed and moved the drink to her mouth, watching Canis intently.

Canis downed the liquid in one motion, wiped his mouth on his sleeve, and moved closer to her. He started feeling dizzy.

"Are you feeling yourself?" Queen Pallanex asked. She moved away from him.

He wiped the sweat from his forehead. "What was in the drink?"

"I do not know what you are talking about," Queen Pallanex answered, staying out of his reach.

The old man stumbled toward his sword. Canis stuck a finger in his throat and purged some of the drink from his body.

Queen Pallanex ran for the door. She ran out of the room and away from the palace. Marcus, Darius, Freya, and their friend barged into the chamber room. Canis was stumbling about, losing his sight and stability. Darius and Freya ran to support their father and king while Marcus gave chase to Queen Pallanex.

Marcus caught up with her at the edge of a bridge overlooking a jagged precipice.

"Why?" Marcus yelled, approaching her like an angry lion.

She tried to soften him with her charm. She could see in his eyes that it was not going to work. "I did it in the name of my elderess, the Elderess Eryx. Your father was a fool to ignore her blessings."

He slammed his sword into her abdomen. Queen Pallanex doubled over but rose up to claw at him. Marcus raked his sword across her throat. "Where is your elderess now?" He tossed her body off the bridge.

"Whoa, wait, Marcus killed her in cold blood?" Julie asked. "How could he do that?"

"It was his way of life then," Redderick Bobo answered. "She had just tried to have him, his brother, and his sister killed and tried to kill his father. What would you expect him to do?"

"I don't know," she said, her eyes tearing up.

"May I finish?"

"Yes, I guess."

The death of Queen Pallanex was the opportunity the untethered essence of Eryx was waiting for--a loyal servant and follower sacrificed for Eryx's cause. Eryx took possession of Queen Pallanex's body. After a thousand years of being without a vessel, her power had drained nearly to non-existence. Only enough remained to revive

Queen Pallanex from the dead, but she now grows ever more powerful the longer she resides--"

"Wait!" Julie interrupted again. "You're telling me Queen Pallanex is really dead, and she has a powerful, angry angel inside of her?"

"Yes." Redderick nodded.

"And you want me to what? Defeat her? Kill her?"

"Yes," he answered again.

"How in the world am I supposed to do that?" Julie asked slowly and carefully, making sure he understood what she was asking.

"You haven't been paying attention, my dear."

"Yes, I have."

"Julie, my child, you have the blood of Tolth running through your veins. That is why you are here. Only one born of angel blood can destroy an angel. Tolth and Ostram could not do it after all they had been through with Eryx, but they needed to send someone to Seras who could. That would be you. Tolth and Ostram sacrificed themselves to give you the power and the training to end Queen Pallanex and in doing so end Eryx and her sinful plans. They gave you the tools, the three gifts. They arranged for Marcus the Solia Custor to find you and train you."

"But I don't want to kill anyone!" Julie covered her face.

"That, my girl, is your chosen path. You are the Betrothed."

"The what? The Betrothed? What is that? I thought I was the Heart?"

Redderick Bobo stammered nervously.

"What aren't you telling me?" Julie asked loudly.

The immortal paused. She could tell he was contemplating lying to her.

"Don't lie to me. You've already told me you expect me to kill someone." She stood up and looked at him deep in the eyes, then screamed, "Why did you call me the Betrothed?"

About the Author

Joe Evener is a fantasy writer located in Sunbury, Ohio where he lives with his wife of thirty plus years. He is a father, grandfather, 5th grade teacher and high school girls' track and field coach. *The Heart of Seras: The Elders* is the second book in the *Heart of Seras* series.

Also by the Author
at Rogue Phoenix Press

Journey to Seras
The Heart of Seras: Book One

Julie Ayers is a normal fifteen year old living in the quiet town of Sunset, Ohio. Her world is turned upside down by the arrival of the school's new teacher, Marcus Campbell.

Marcus Campbell has a secret. He is a warrior from a medieval dimension searching for the mythical "Heart"-a hero given to the people of Seras to rid their world of impending evil. Marcus's quest is challenged when he realizes that the "Heart" is the vibrant teenage girl. Now, against his better judgment, he must try convincing Julie to go to his world and begin preparation to face whatever evil lies ahead.

Journey to Seras is the first book in the six part *The Heart of Seras* fantasy series. It begins the adventures of the two unlikely heroes as they battle the dark forces of Seras

VISIT OUR WEBSITE
FOR THE FULL INVENTORY
OF QUALITY BOOKS:

http://www.roguephoenixpress.com

Representing Excellence in Publishing

Quality trade paperbacks and downloads
in multiple formats,
in genres ranging from historical
to contemporary romance, mystery and science fiction.
Visit the website then bookmark it.
We add new titles each month!

www.ingramcontent.com/pod-product-compliance
Lightning Source LLC
Chambersburg PA
CBHW060210180626
46813CB00007B/2766